The Ghost
and Christie McFee

The Ghost

and Christie McFee

A Cozy Ghost Mystery

Suzanne Stengl

Publisher: Mya & Angus
Cover Design: April Martinez

Also published as GHOSTLY TREASURE

www.suzannestengl.com

MYA & ANGUS

Acknowledgments

Thank you to my beta readers: Roxy Boroughs, C.J. Carmichael, Victoria Chatham, Brenda M. Collins, Amy Jo Fleming, Marlene Renee and A.M. Westerling.

And, as always, thank you to all the Banditos at Bandit Creek Books for your encouragement and support.

Dedication

To Tawny Stokes

for her enthusiasm!

Prologue

Bandit Creek, Montana
August 2012

The gold had lain at the bottom of Lost Lake for over a hundred years, tempting treasure hunters and shattering dreams. Rumors had spread about the lost gold shipment and divers had perished searching for it. With each year that passed, the strength of the legend had grown, bringing new hopefuls, more *freak* accidents, and more deaths.

Ethel Hamilton tucked a pin into the bun that held her hair, adjusted her hat and shook out her long skirt. Then she picked up the sandy piece of newspaper and watched the young man come out of the dive shack. He walked across the beach toward the dock.

She looked at the newspaper and, one more time, read the headline printed on the first page of the *Bandit Creek Gazette*. "Diver almost drowns searching for Lost Lake treasure." She dropped the paper, letting it fall back on the beach.

It was time she did something about that gold.

Chapter One

Gaven St. Michel saw the loose page of newspaper fluttering across the beach. He caught it, tossed it in the trash can and walked onto the dock to wait for the divers to board *La Bonne Aventure*.

Some days he hated the tourists, but they were his job, at least for the summer. He didn't have to do this for the rest of his life.

Looking at his clipboard, he saw seven names. Charlie had booked them yesterday, and checked their credentials.

Except, sometimes, Charlie skimped on the credentials. His Uncle Charlie was always glad for the money from the tourists and never wanted to turn anyone away. But some of these people had no business being on a dive boat. Hopefully, there wouldn't be any situations this morning.

They trooped out of the dive shack, carrying their masks, snorkels and fins. The air tanks, wet suits, BCDs and regulators were already on the boat.

An older couple approached first—the couple from Missoula. They looked to be in their late fifties. They'd dived in lots of places, most recently last February in the Galapagos, so they were obviously experienced and wouldn't be a problem. He'd help them with their time and depth limits since they probably weren't used to diving at altitude.

A younger couple followed, holding hands. The newlyweds from Seattle . . . not as experienced but they'd had the basic PADI courses.

Ripley and Terrence trailed behind the newlyweds. The teenage boys from Bandit Creek. He'd taken them out several times already this summer. Those kids would be Divemasters before too long.

He greeted the divers and sent them to get ready. Six of them. There was supposed to be a seventh—a woman from San Francisco. He glanced at his clipboard.

Christie McFee, the last name on the list. No experience listed, but Charlie had scribbled one word. *Trained.*

Gaven clenched his jaw. That meant Charlie had taken her to the pool at the Community Center. He would have given her a brief orientation there. That was all. Warm water and perfect conditions.

Please God, don't let today be her first open water experience. Not a hot August morning in a seven mil wet suit.

He'd have to buddy with her, which meant his attention would be pulled from the group.

But the boys, Ripley and Terrence, had done the dive to the Old Town a dozen times or more. They'd be able to help with guiding. And Gaven would be able to keep an eye on the new diver.

He glanced at his watch. A few minutes past nine. Maybe she wouldn't show up.

No such luck. He saw the white Chevy Cobalt pull into the dirt parking lot beside Charlie's Dive Shack. A Missoula Airport sticker decorated the rear window of the car.

According to his clipboard, the woman lived in San Francisco. Why not learn to dive there? Why come all the way to Lost Lake to do your first dive?

He shook his head. It wasn't his job to figure out why the tourists did what they did. His job was to keep them safe while they did it.

And if he hadn't needed the money, he wouldn't be here.

The driver's door opened and an attractive young woman stepped out of the car, wearing sunglasses, a loose, long sleeved top, baggy shorts and sandals.

She was about five foot six, maybe five seven. Her long brown hair wisped around her shoulders and, judging by the tan on those long legs, she'd been outdoors a lot this summer. Beneath the baggy clothes, she looked shapely, but . . . thin. Maybe a little too thin, like she'd recently been sick.

He couldn't read her expression. She looked like she was holding on to her feelings, keeping them tight. At any rate, she didn't seem particularly excited about this trip.

She carried a net bag of mask, snorkel and fins. With her attention focused on the other divers who were pulling on their neoprene, she stepped onto the dock.

"Good morning," he said. "I'm Gaven St. Michel. I'm your Divemaster."

"I . . . I don't want to wear a wet suit."

Not very friendly. Not even a *good morning*. "You're Christie McFee?"

"Yes. But nobody said anything about wearing a wet suit. It's too hot."

He heard his sigh, a loud one, and right at this moment he didn't care about putting on his public face. "You're up in the mountains, lady. The water is sixty-three degrees. You wear neoprene."

She gulped and her tanned face seemed to pale. "One of those hoods too?"

"If you want to be comfortable. We'll be down about forty minutes."

"I . . . I don't like the hoods. They feel claustrophobic."

Somebody'd put her up to this. Somebody wanted her to learn to dive. Never a good scenario.

"Have you ever dived before?"

"Yes."

"Where?"

"In Bandit Creek. In the pool. With that guy from the store."

Great. Why did Charlie do this to him? "How much do you weigh?"

"What?"

"Nothing personal. You need weights, remember? I need to know what to put on your weight belt."

She looked confused. "Uh, in the pool, he gave me—"

"The neoprene is buoyant. You need more weight than you did in the pool."

She nodded, like she'd just remembered that much. And then she told him how much she weighed.

He was right. She *was* too thin. He wanted to ask her if she'd been sick, but he didn't. Instead he said, "Tell me the five steps before entry."

He saw her go inside her head, pull out the information, and recite the steps. She knew them. Intellectually, at least.

"You're out of air."

"I am?"

He paused, wondering if she was for real. Maybe Charlie had sent her as a test. "*If* you are out of air," Gaven said. "Give me the hand signal."

She gave him the correct hand signal.

He quizzed her on a few more hand signals. She seemed ready and she was probably safe enough, but for some reason, he had a bad feeling about this.

"I'm your buddy. Stay close to me. No more than six feet. Come on."

Gaven walked down the dock and stepped onto the boat. Then he turned and waited for her to board. She glanced around as if looking for something to hold on to. She'd probably never been on a boat.

He held out his hand to help her and she put her small hand in his. The air temperature was already over eighty, but her hand felt cold.

He guided her to a bench beside the Seattle newlyweds and she sat. Then he found his smallest wet suit and brought it to her. "Put this on."

She paused a moment, like she wanted to argue. And then she accepted it.

Right. It was definitely not her idea to go diving. Or, maybe it was one of those bucket list things. Something she'd decided she had to do in her lifetime. Except, most people didn't make a bucket list until they were a lot older. She was too young for a bucket list.

It was something else.

"Yo!"

Charlie ambled down to the dock, eating a ham

sandwich. With all the fat he'd accumulated over the years, his Uncle Charlie Beauregard could probably last down there for an hour without a wet suit.

Charlie had turned forty-one last Wednesday. A week ago today. The two of them had celebrated at the Powder Horn Saloon and Charlie had talked about how happy he was to have Gaven working for him over the summer ... and would he consider staying on over the winter for the snowmobile and dog sled tours.

Gaven, of course, had said no.

"You checked her out?" he asked his uncle.

"She'll be fine."

"This is her first open water."

"I said she'll be fine. She's a quick study."

Gaven closed his eyes for a moment. If it was up to him, he wouldn't take her. Not with the group.

He looked over to where she sat. Watched as she took off her clothes, and—he'd been right—all that baggy clothing hid a shapely body. She wore a one-piece navy bathing suit.

"Is it true about the legend?" the newlywed woman asked.

The woman from the older couple looked up. "What legend?"

Christie McFee shook out her wet suit and started to pull it on.

"There's a legend," Charlie said, neatly slipping

into his spiel. "When the Old Town of Bandit Creek flooded in 1911, the miners left gold behind. Many have tried to find it. Several have come close. But anyone who tries to take the gold . . . dies."

Charlie paused in his chatter, waiting for the attention of his audience.

It was a stupid legend to perpetuate. But it might keep the tourists from poking around the Old Town too much. If they wanted to go into the submerged buildings, they'd think twice. Maybe.

Of course, the legend had not stopped the wreck divers, many of whom had come back with artifacts of the Old Town and sold them. Someone had even found books and gave them to the Bandit Creek Library for restoration.

"Are the buildings still standing?" the newlywed man asked.

"Most of them," Charlie answered.

"Why don't they rot?"

"Same reason shipwrecks don't rot," Charlie said. "Especially in freshwater lakes, like this one. The wood will be preserved. Even in sea water, as long as the salinity is low, the old wooden ships have lasted for centuries."

"Sweet," Ripley and Terrence said in unison, like they always did. The boys had heard Charlie's tourist patter at least a dozen times.

"How did the town flood?" The woman from the older couple wanted to know.

"Landslide," Charlie answered. "Off Crow

Mountain. The rubble dammed the creek back in 1911."

"And everybody in the town died," Ripley said, like he always did.

"Not everybody," Charlie carried on. "Many got out in time, but a lot of lives were lost."

"And their ghosts still haunt Lost Lake," Terrence said, like *he* always did.

The teenagers got into the spirit of the tour. Charlie didn't even have to pay them. Although, he did give them a discounted rate for diving.

"Nowadays—" Charlie went on with his talk, "—we're learning a lot about flooded forests. With hydroelectric dams, a lot of timber is submerged. It's never been economically feasible to cut down the trees before building the dam, but now, some efforts are being made to harvest the timber underwater."

"Is that wood any good?" the man from the older couple asked.

"As good as new," Charlie said. "It's the bacteria that eat the wood. There's very little oxygen in the lake water for bacteria to survive. Some flooded forests contain premium wood."

"Can we take anything from the town?" the newlywed man asked.

"Not unless you want the ghosts to get you," Ripley said.

"The Bandit Creek Ladies Historical Society is working to have the Old Town declared a national historic site," Charlie said. "Most of the artifacts recovered from the Old Town are in the museum at the Town Hall. Be sure to stop by. It's open from one until five every afternoon."

"I think this is too small," Christie McFee said, as she struggled into her neoprene.

"Needs to be tight, girl," Charlie told her. "Fills with water. If you have too much water inside, your body can't heat it and you'll be cold."

Gaven pulled his uncle aside. "She doesn't want to dive."

"She's just a little anxious," Charlie said. "She did fine in the pool. Normal to be anxious for your first time out." He took another bite of his sandwich, and then, talking with his mouth full, he added, "Loosen up, boy. Ya worry too much."

Christie squeezed her eyes shut and willed herself to take slow, calming breaths. The air temperature was at least eighty degrees, the sun beat down on them, and she was wearing this horrible, sweltering, tight wet suit.

Charlie, the older man, stood at the wheel, *not* wearing a wet suit. That probably meant he would not dive with them. He would stay on board. It made sense that someone would stay with the boat. But she'd never done this before, so she had no idea what would happen.

As Charlie guided the boat to the center of the

lake, he kept talking about the old Bandit Creek, about 1911, and the landslide damming the creek. And the water level rising over several days, and the Old Town now forty-eight feet underwater. And something about it all being preserved because the water was cold and because there was little oxygen. Who cared?

She tugged at the hood under her chin trying to let a sliver of breeze touch her skin and praying today would soon be over.

Charlie rambled on, giving them a variation of the story she'd read in the *Bandit Creek Gazette* when she'd searched online. About the gold left behind by the miners.

Gold was treasure. This dive qualified as diving for treasure.

Suddenly she felt water splash over her face and seep into the neck opening of her hood, trailing a cool path inside the wet suit. Blessed cold and refreshing water.

"More?" the younger man asked her. She couldn't remember what he'd said his name was.

"Please."

She held her face up while he poured water over her head. He didn't have his hood on yet. A slight breeze sifted through his dark hair.

"Anybody else?"

The older woman asked for a splash of water. Everyone else was tolerating the heat.

"I'm okay," one of the teenage boys said.

"Me too," the other one said. "We're almost above the Old Town now."

Then the engine cut and the boat stopped traveling, and started bobbing in the water . . . in a nauseating rocking motion.

The younger man, the Divemaster, was talking. "Check your buddy's equipment. Make sure you have enough air in your BCD for the surface. Charlie will help you." The group paired off, each going through what looked like a standard checklist.

"Christie and I will go first," the Divemaster said. "When we're all in the water, give me the Okay signal. Then we'll descend together."

"Hey, Gaven," one of the teenagers called out. "Is it all right if Terrence and I lead the way into the Old Town?"

"You can lead," Gaven said. "But don't get too far ahead." He continued with his instructions. "We'll be at an average depth of forty-eight feet for about forty minutes. Stay close to your buddy and keep everyone in sight. None of you are qualified as wreck divers so don't go inside the buildings."

"Yeah, the ghosts hate it when you do that. A couple of weeks ago, there was a guy out here who—"

"That's enough, Ripley." Gaven cut off the story.

She hadn't read anything about a diving accident. And she didn't want to know.

"All set?" Gaven asked, speaking just to her.

Her heartbeat pounded in her ears. "I think so," she said, still sitting on the bench, trying to focus on the horizon, trying to stop the nausea she felt with the pitching boat.

He clamped an air tank to a vest—the BCD—that's what Charlie had called it. "Stand up."

She did, holding the back of the bench with one hand, balancing herself as the boat swayed.

Gaven slipped a yellow weight belt around her waist. "Right-hand release, remember?" He bent his head to look in her eyes. She turned away. She didn't want him to see how scared she was.

There was so much to remember. She felt him take her hand, her right hand, and gently place it over the weight belt buckle.

"Try it."

She did and the heavy weight belt released easily. It would have fallen on her toes if he hadn't been holding it.

He refastened it. Then he lifted the air tank and clunked it on the bench. "Sit here," he said, guiding her into position in front of the tank.

He was helping her with the vest—the BCD—adjusting buckles, tightening straps. Doing all the things she should have known how to do. Maybe it would have been better to take a course first, but she hadn't wanted to waste the time, since she'd never do this again.

She heard a hiss of air as he pressed the valve

on her BCD, slightly inflating her vest.

"You really want to dive?"

"I do," she answered, looking at the deck. She heard his sigh, and knew he had doubts about taking her into the water.

He waited for a long moment, like he was deciding something. And then he said, "Did you have any trouble equalizing in the pool?"

"You mean my ears?" She glanced up briefly, and then averted her eyes.

Yesterday, she'd managed to get to the bottom of the pool when Charlie was teaching her. Nine feet . . . and she was standing up, so not really nine feet. Her ears had hurt the whole time. How was she ever going to go down to forty-eight feet?

"My ears hurt a little," she lied, speaking to the deck of the boat, still not looking at him.

"Charlie probably told you to equalize every three feet but you'll do it more often." The tone of his voice had changed, slightly. "Every foot, or even every half foot. Signal me if your ears hurt." He paused. "You know how to make a Something-is-Wrong signal?"

It was a signal she definitely knew. She showed him.

"All right. You're ready. Stand up."

She did, bracing her legs in a wide stance, trying to balance on the rocking boat. Why did the equipment have to be so heavy?

"Once we're in the water, you'll hold on to me," Gaven said.

Something about his voice reassured her. He sounded calm, and in charge, and . . . kind. Maybe everything would be all right.

"I'll release all the air in your BCD and I'll control our descent. Got that?"

"Yes."

"Okay," he said. "Put on your mask."

She did, feeling the seal tighten around her face. Then she could feel his fingers touch her face as he adjusted the mask.

"Pinch your nose," he said, putting her hand in place. "And blow."

It was the easy way to equalize, apparently . . . if it worked. Charlie had said something about yawning, and swallowing, and various other ways of clearing her ears. But, in the short time she'd experimented, she hadn't been able to do anything that would relieve the pressure.

"You have to look at me," Gaven said.

And now besides being calm and kind and reassuring, there was a touch of humor in his voice. Or, maybe she imagined it.

"Watch my eyes."

She did. Trying to project an image of confidence. Noticing, for the first time, the deep brown of his eyes. The dark fringe of lashes. And, was that . . . concern?

"Every time I nod, you pinch your nose and

blow. Got that?"

"Yes. You nod, I pinch and blow."

"Keep watching me," he said. "All the way down."

The boat bounced and tilted. She reached out and held on to his forearm. He stood solid and strong, and completely unaffected by the movement. But she felt the nausea from the motion, and the weakness from the heat, and the tight claustrophobia of the wet suit. The mask was even worse, trapping her, forcing her to breathe through her mouth.

"Slow down your breathing." He put the regulator in her mouth and she felt like she was suffocating.

"Breathe in slowly," he said, waiting for her to do that. "And now breathe out, completely. Count if that helps."

She heard the flow of the air as she breathed in . . . and out . . . testing the regulator before she was underwater.

But she wanted to rip out the regulator and rip off her mask, and her hood. And every piece of equipment she was wearing. She wanted to forget about diving. She wanted to give up.

"Don't worry about running out of air. I'll keep an eye on your gauges."

Right. The gauges. She was supposed to keep an eye on her gauges, and remember to breathe. And remember to breathe slowly. And search for treasure. And not suffocate.

Gaven guided her to the platform. In her peripheral vision, she noticed Charlie setting an air tank and BCD on the floor of the platform.

Gaven's equipment. Charlie had set it up for him. And then Gaven was quickly donning his own BCD and air tank.

"Lift your foot, girl," Charlie said. He slipped a fin over her neoprene boot, and then the other. "Okay, you're ready."

She wasn't ready. She focused on breathing, on getting her air from a tank strapped to her back, and she felt panic. Then she heard Gaven's voice, as he stood beside her.

"Put your hand over your mask and regulator. Like this," he said, moving her hand into position.

Good idea. Otherwise she'd probably dislodge her mask or regulator, or both, when she splashed down.

"You're going to take a big step out and that's it. I'll see you in the water. Ready?"

She stood on the platform that floated about four feet above the lake's surface, and she heard her heart thudding in her ears. She listened to the sound of her breaths coming through the regulator.

"On three, you step out," Gaven said. "One . . . two . . . three."

She tried not to think about it. Clamping her hand over her mask and regulator, she took a giant stride. As she dropped into the water, she prayed she would survive this experience.

Chapter Two

The water effervesced with tiny white bubbles and, all in an instant, quiet and cold relief closed in on her. The heat was gone, and the nausea was gone. She heard herself breathing as she inhaled the air through her regulator, heard the hiss of inflow, and then the gurgle as she exhaled.

The storm of white bubbles dissipated, and only a trail of small clear air bubbles from her breathing remained, twinkling up to the surface like the wave of a magic wand.

Floating directly in front of her was a little fish, about a foot long. Sunlight sparkled on its green speckled head and pinkish-red gills, and its sleek body gleamed, showing off bluish-green silver, dotted with black spots. A horizontal pink stripe streaked along its sides, flashing in the reflection from the surface.

Fluttering its whispery fins, the fish seemed to study her, as if it was deciding whether or not she was capable of entering its world.

The water exploded with bubbles again, boiling all around her. If the fish stayed, she couldn't see it. And then Gaven was in front of her, hovering. He held out his hand in the Okay signal.

She returned the signal, surprising herself, as she realized, she really was okay. At least for the moment.

The other divers were splashing down, one after the other, circling her and Gaven. They each gave him the Okay signal. Then he took hold of her vest and pulled her to him.

Taking her hand, he put it on the strap of his BCD vest. She slipped her fingers underneath and held on, focusing on the black fabric glistening in the water.

She felt him touch her chin, lifting her head up to look at his eyes. His deep brown reassuring eyes.

He put her other hand over her mask. She'd forgot about that, about being ready to pinch her nose. There was so much to remember. She was aware of him adjusting her BCD. He would be releasing the air so she could go down, and she knew she would drop slowly because he would control their speed.

He looked away a moment, giving the other

divers the signal to descend.

And panic raced into her thoughts. She had to go down to forty-eight feet. She couldn't do it. She—

Then he was watching her again, and she saw nothing but his eyes. He nodded. So she pinched her nose and blew against the pressure, even though there wasn't any pressure, not yet. They were still just beneath the surface.

Maybe he wanted to make sure she knew what to do?

They moved down a few feet, and she felt the pressure in her ears, that same pain, not too bad, but there. She took her hand away from her mask and signaled Something-is-Wrong.

Immediately he ascended, maybe three feet, she wasn't sure.

Then the pain was gone. For now. But—but—she couldn't do this. She knew she couldn't—

He nodded, giving her that signal again. The pain was already gone, but she pinched her nose anyway and blew.

He nodded again, so she pinched her nose and blew, even though everything was still clear. *Why did he want her to clear again?*

She didn't know, but she followed his instructions as she held on to his vest and watched his eyes.

He continued the drill of nodding, and waiting for her to clear. She didn't need to clear, but she pinched and blew anyway.

Maybe he was getting her to practice?

Then, although there wasn't any pressure in her ears, she realized they must be descending, because the water felt cooler on her face and hands, and the light was dimming from the hot August day in the world above them.

Don't think about it. Not about the possibility of pain. Not about the claustrophobia. Not about the fish. She forced herself to focus on the repetition. He nodded. She pinched her nose, gently blew against the pressure. And she watched his eyes.

At first, it seemed intrusive to focus on his eyes like that. Then it didn't matter. She noticed that she liked watching his eyes, that they were a remarkable color of warm chocolate.

All of a sudden, something changed. For the first time since they'd left the surface, Gaven looked away from her. She followed his gaze, seeing the other six divers drifting in a circle around them. And . . . she saw a tree, with barren dark branches reaching into the orange-tinted depths.

A tree.

Feeling a surge of euphoria and relief, she realized they had made it. All the way down.

The other divers hung suspended about three feet off the bottom. She let go of Gaven's vest, dropped, and felt her fins touch the floor of the lake, sending up a puff of silt to swirl around her legs.

Gaven adjusted her BCD, and then she was floating above the sandy bottom, feeling like an angel gliding, and oddly confident . . . almost giddy with the exhilaration of what she'd done.

She'd made it. They were on the bottom of Lost Lake. Forty-eight feet below the surface and her ears didn't hurt. She'd actually made it.

Her sister would be proud.

Gaven watched as Christie waved her fins and moved smoothly through the water. Charlie was right. She was a quick study.

On the boat, she'd looked like she might back out, but she was determined—for somebody who seemed afraid of diving. He still couldn't figure out *why* she wanted to dive, but . . . she had pretty eyes.

The prettiest shade of hazel and green he'd ever seen. Kind of shy, and vibrant, and sexy.

As they'd descended, she'd gradually become calmer.

Now she seemed excited as she whirled around in the hazy water, trying to see everything at once—the school of whitefish flashing through the branches of the bare deciduous trees, the goldeye with their flat silvery bodies, the cutthroat trout and the golden trout. And today, there were even a few rainbows.

Ripley and Terrence had drifted over to the

sign. Christie spotted it and swam to join them. The two couples followed her.

The sign consisted of a tilted board nailed on a four-by-four post. One end of the board had been sawed straight. The other end was broken, so the sign formed a directional arrow. In haphazard strokes, white block letters on the grayed wood said *Bandit Creek*.

The sign was a recent addition to the underwater Bandit Creek.

Last summer, Charlie had mounted the post in a tub of concrete and buried it in the sand, heaping rocks around the base to disguise the recent digging. His uncle had taken great care to make the white letters look as though they were carelessly written.

Gaven hadn't told anyone about the age of the sign and he didn't feel right about letting them think it was authentic. However, the rest of the town was authentic . . . unless Ripley and Terrence had added something. Again.

He looked for them, remembering some of their pranks, and wondered what to do about the boys and their enthusiasm.

Then the newlywed woman handed him her camera.

He waited for all the divers—the newlyweds, the older couple, Ripley and Terrence, and Christie—to gather around the sign for the picture. With Ripley stretched out along the sandy bottom in front of the group, Terrence hung upside down above everyone.

Gaven took the photo. It would probably end up on the bulletin board in the dive shack.

As he handed the camera back to the woman, he signaled to Ripley and Terrence. The usual—you lead, I'll follow. They turned and slowly glided away. The other four divers slipped in behind them.

But Christie held on to the sign, going hand over hand until she reached its bottom. She lifted up a rock, like she was ready to pull all the heavy rocks away and have a look at the base.

Could she tell the wood was new? And how come she wasn't keeping an eye on the others? He'd thought she'd be timid and keep close to the group.

Maybe not. Now that she was over her equalization problems, she'd immersed herself in the adventure and seemed completely confident.

Maybe, a little overconfident.

He'd better hold on to her. She was brushing her hand over the four-by-four post. He moved closer and touched her chin with one finger, lifting it up to get her attention. Then he clasped his hands palm to palm. The signal that meant—hold hands.

Instantly, she forgot about the post, reached out and took his hand, settling her palm against his, like she trusted him.

That felt nice.

. . . . .

Charlie had anchored the boat so they'd enter the town from the northeast, as they usually did for this tour. The First Time Tour. Since Ripley and Terrence had done it several times, they knew their way through the trees to the starting point.

A few minutes later, the group reached the windmill that stood like a lone sentinel guarding the entrance to the Old Town. Its blades turned slightly in the lake currents. Nearby, another windmill had crashed to the ground, its blades half-buried in the silt.

Christie made a movement to swim up to the turning blades, but Gaven held her back. Surprising him, she pulled out of his grasp. He swam in front of her, motioned for her to look at him, and then pointed to his watch. She seemed to understand.

If she touched everything, they'd never finish the tour in the allotted time. He held out his hand and she took it. Together they floated over the half-buried windmill and reached the street sign that said Stokes Road. This sign really was authentic.

Ripley and Terrence hovered at either end of the sign, pointing to it. If the others remembered Charlie's talk, this was the part where he'd said they'd enter the town at Stokes Road—named after one of the early founders of Bandit Creek.

From there, they skimmed over the horse corrals and reached the end of Main Street. Tall and gloomy, the building fronts butted against each other. Boardwalks lined the street and the hitching posts stood strong and sturdy.

Much of the debris that had peppered the bottom of the lake had been gathered by the treasure hunters, but not all of it. As they journeyed past the stables, they saw some rusted buckets and a steel wagon wheel with five spokes. A few bottles with flat sides poked up out of the silt—clear glass, green glass, and even blue glass.

The volunteers had lined up many undamaged bottles and dishes on the shelves in the museum but, Gaven knew, there were also complete pieces inside the buildings.

They remained because the treasure hunters didn't care about old bottles and dishes. They searched for gold, not antiques, and that was a good thing. Otherwise the town would have been stripped long ago. At any rate, much of the town remained as it was on the days the floodwaters rose in late November of 1911.

Back then, there was mostly horse traffic, and horse and buggy. Only a few cars. Most of those cars had made it out in time. Some had not. Now the rusting cars and dilapidated buggies scattered along the street, resting in the places where the flood had deposited them, like the buckboard snugged against the hitching post in front of the

Last Chance Saloon.

Next door, in front of the Blacksmith's Shop, a flatbed wagon had been abandoned with its load of barrels. Barrels without lids—pried off by the treasure hunters as they'd scavenged for the legendary gold.

The newlywed couple peered inside the Blacksmith's Shop, pausing at the entrance, hopefully remembering his instructions to stay outside. From where they floated, they'd be able to see the forge and the anvils and some of the abandoned tools, the hammers and vises.

Further down Main Street, Ripley and Terrence waited for the group, circling above the carriage that sat marooned in the middle of the road.

Christie jerked his hand, squeezing hard. Then she clutched his arm with both hands as she stared across the street at Maggie O'Connor's Boarding House.

Movement caught his eye, on the second floor ... the faded checkered curtains fluttering in the light currents through the open window. She must have been paying attention to Charlie's ghost stories.

Taking hold of one of her hands, he held it in both of his, wanting to reassure her, and he waited for her to calm down again. When she realized what she'd seen was only curtains, she ducked her head. She must have been embarrassed. Pulling her hand away, she swam to where the newlyweds looked through the door of the Blacksmith's Shop.

She would be sufficiently spooked now to stay out of the buildings and he wouldn't worry about her going inside. The last thing he needed was one of his tourists getting their equipment tangled up inside a door or under a ceiling.

Outside of Maggie O'Connor's Boarding House, the older couple inspected the hanging sign over the boardwalk. A brightly painted piece of wood suspended from two thick chains off a beam above the door. It would have been easy to spot as travelers came up the street from the train station.

They continued toward the carriage where Ripley and Terrence pretended to drive. All along the street, the tall false fronts looked down on them, many with empty windows. Some of the windows wore shutters. Others held pieces of glass, probably broken when the floodwaters advanced.

As they floated past Garvey's Saloon, the half door swung faintly, like a patron had just entered.

Across from Garvey's, the building had a stoop attached to the front. Although the stoop leaned, the rest of the building stood tall and solid. A school of cutthroat trout flickered out the empty second story window.

By now, they'd caught up with Ripley and Terrence, and they all drifted past the newspaper office, called the *Bandit Creek Gazette* even then.

The signs on the buildings helped to tell the

story of old Bandit Creek. Some of them were simple, and some were more elaborate. Like the one above the Powder Horn Saloon.

The Powder Horn had probably been the most popular drinking establishment of its day. It was the only saloon that had been recreated when Bandit Creek was rebuilt downstream.

The Men's Club, with its second floor balcony, stood next to the Powder Horn. From that balcony, a person could see much of what happened on the Main Street of the town.

This was a part of the story Charlie loved to tell. The high class establishment boasted a Men's Club from the front but—from the back—it was a brothel.

As the stories went, this brothel's clientele consisted of wealthy men in town, and many of them lived in the mansions on the River Road. These mansions backed onto a lane, the same lane that ran behind the Main Street buildings.

The men could slip into the laneway behind their homes, cross over to the Men's Club, and climb the back stairs to the rooms used by the prostitutes. The fact that the Men's Club was a brothel was one of the worst kept secrets in Bandit Creek.

Gaven checked for Christie, and noticed she was staying close to the older couple. She was supposed to be with him, but she probably felt embarrassed about mistaking the waving curtains for a ghost. At least, she hadn't had to deal with—

As he had the thought, he was proved wrong. A huge white sheet burst out from the second floor balcony, causing the newlyweds, the older couple and Christie to tighten together in alarm.

Ripley and Terrence were up to their tricks again. They must have rigged the sheet like a sling shot. Now, the huge whiteness floated ominously above the street, and then slowly began to settle.

Ripley and Terrence swam to the side, out of the way.

As the puff of white floated down, the older couple looked at each other, shrugged and moved aside. The newlyweds nodded, looked at Ripley and Terrence and also got out of the way.

Only Christie hadn't figured it out yet. Dropping to the lake floor, she curled up in a ball.

Her first diving trip would be memorable.

Gaven pointed to the boys, they understood, and gathered up the sheet. He swam over to Christie and tried to get her attention, but she had her eyes squeezed shut. He tapped her hand. She flinched. Then he took her hand in his, hoping she would recognize his touch.

She did, opening those beautiful hazel green eyes. He pointed to the boys who were standing on their heads with the sheet bundled in their arms— the pose they used to suggest their unconcern. Any other time, it would have been funny, but at the moment he was worried about frightening a new diver. One who was already uneasy.

Letting herself rise from the bottom, she held on to his hand and watched the boys. Then, as if finally understanding it wasn't a ghost, she closed her eyes briefly, and pulled away from him.

Between the curtains and the sheet, it was too much.

Gaven decided he would have to do something about the boys. They loved the idea of ghosts in the Old Town, but he couldn't have them scaring a new diver.

With the commotion over, they traveled past the bank, past Mather & Son General Store, past Howard Massey's Harness Shop. And the Sheriff's Office and the jail and the Town Hall.

Finally they came to the Opera House—home of the famous singer, Jo-Jo Sullivan. Charlie's research said her voice was so beautiful she was called the Siren of Bandit Creek.

Last on the tour, they stopped at the Train Station where the divers could look inside the windows and see the telegraph office. They could float above the rusted tracks of the Montana Northern and see the graveyard beyond. But that was a tour for another day.

The newlywed woman had her camera out again, photographing her husband, with fins and arms crossed, as he leaned against the door to the telegraph office. The older couple hovered six feet higher, studying the sign above the door.

Ripley and Terrence sat in the Model T Ford parked out front and, like they did with the carriage, they pretended to drive it. Charlie had told the group it was a 1908 five passenger touring car. An impressive vehicle back in the day. Not so impressive now, with its folded canvas roof in tatters, the strips of material moving in the slight current.

He looked around for Christie, thinking she might be interested in the car. But she wasn't up the street in front of the Opera House. She wasn't inside the telegraph office. She wasn't across the train tracks.

Not a sign of her. Not even a trail of exhaled air bubbles. Panic lumped in his throat.

A little rainbow trout wandered out of the second story window of the train station, crossed the tracks and disappeared in the direction of the graveyard.

Chapter Three

The tone of her air bubbles had changed. They made an almost tinkling sound, like a crystal chandelier shaking in a small tremor. The road curved past the old graveyard, and around the bend, another road branched off to the right.

This way. This way. This way.

The voice echoed through her thoughts. A woman's voice. She'd heard it earlier, but, obviously, it couldn't be a voice since she was underwater. So, not a voice. It was more like an idea, a fixation, a need to follow this road.

The road branched again, and as she started to swim toward it, she felt the current push at her. And then lift her, suddenly sweeping her back toward the graveyard, like she was a tiny bug swatted by a giant.

Tumbling, she dropped, spinning like a top until she crashed to the bottom of the lake and landed on her hands and knees in front of a three-foot high wooden headstone. She exhaled and heard the shiny ringing sound of her breathing and, as she inhaled, her body lifted above the ground so she was floating over the headstone ... over a whole field of headstones.

Some were wooden and some were made of concrete. Or maybe it was limestone—she didn't know. But whatever the material, it had flaked away in parts and the inscriptions had faded to be almost unreadable. She made out a few dates. One was 1899, another 1901, and two others said 1895.

Before she could read more, the current swept through the graveyard, lifting the silt like a sandstorm and she couldn't see.

Don't worry. I won't let him hurt you.

The woman's voice was back in her head. But she knew that was crazy. Crazy, but it didn't matter. Nothing mattered. Except, she liked listening to the melodic ring of her breathing.

From some dim part of her brain, she knew she felt dizzy, like she was spinning again in the whirling silt, but somehow she didn't care. It was like being drunk and untroubled. Then the silt settled and she could see again ... and she saw a figure about six gravestones ahead of her.

Another trick set up by the teenagers. And this

was a poor one. If they were trying to scare her, they needed to do better.

It was a mannequin dressed in a long gray coat, made to look like a man about forty years old. It had shoulder length blond hair, thinning at the top, a closely trimmed beard, and a moustache. The hair waved in the water, sifting over the narrow scowling face.

Beneath the long gray coat, it was dressed in old-fashioned clothes—a shirt and string tie with a vest over top. Dark pants. A shiny belt buckle, and a second buckle—on a holster. The boys had given it a holster. They probably wanted to make it look more authentic, like it belonged in 1911.

The lake currents flapped the coat, exposing a gun on the hip, and a vest. The vest showed the gold chain of a pocket watch, and—this was completely ridiculous—the vest had seven holes, surrounded by dark brown. The boys wanted to make it look like the ghost had been shot.

Not very realistic. *Seven* holes?

All of a sudden, she heard something different. Another voice . . . inside her head.

Surprise filled her as she realized it was her sister's voice. Meghan's voice. Meghan was inside her head, talking to her, from far away. She couldn't make out the words.

Maybe being underwater had some kind of psychotic effect. Maybe she should have learned more about scuba, and what to expect, before taking this—

Christie! Stop analyzing everything and listen to me!

Definitely Meghan's voice. As usual, Meghan sounded frustrated with her. Meghan had always wanted her to stop working, to take time off, to enjoy life and—

Go back, Christie. Gaven is looking for you.

What if he was? He hadn't wanted to take her diving in the first place. He hadn't even bothered to hide his doubts about her ability. But then, he'd been right. She didn't know what she was doing and she'd only wanted to get this over with and move on.

Never mind that Gaven fellow. We have work to do. Competing with her sister's voice, the first voice had returned.

The mannequin shuddered and the water rippled around it, shimmering like a mirage. The mannequin's arms lifted above its head, stretching out, making it look taller. An optical illusion, of course, but pretty well done. She had to give Ripley and Terrence credit.

She could feel the currents again, like a little whirlwind sweeping across the floor of the lake and pushing her back.

The orange haze of the underwater world darkened, and she realized how drowsy she was, how much she wanted to sleep. In the next moment, she felt a yank on the front strap of her BCD, and she felt herself rising. She could see nothing but swirling silt.

Time seemed to slow. Then the orange haze returned and the world grew brighter.

Her hearing changed. The crystal sound of her breathing was gone, replaced by the gasp of air coming in, and a quick hissing out. She tried to focus on her breathing like Gaven had told her to do. Part of her brain knew something wasn't right. A larger part of her brain wrapped her in calmness—a serenity she hadn't known in a long time.

Something was pulling her up. Or someone. She knew she was moving toward the surface because her ears whistled as the pressure changed. No pain, but a change in pressure.

The light grew brighter ... as if the sun had been pulled out of the sky and its intensity aimed right at her.

Warmth spread over her face, as though she was out of the water, but she knew she couldn't be. Drowsiness closed around her. The diving equipment weighed her down.

Christie. Wake up. Gaven has you. You're all right. Wake up, Christie.

It was Meghan again, talking to her inside her head. That same dream. Then the weight of her equipment disappeared, and she felt like she was being lifted.

There were more voices. Different than the ones she'd heard in her head.

"I've called the ambulance. They'll meet us at the dock."

That was Charlie. The older man who'd taken her to the Community Center Pool. He'd taught her how to use the equipment. But what did they need an ambulance for?

"Christie? C'mon, beautiful, open those eyes."

Beautiful? Was someone calling *her* beautiful? No, not her. Meghan was the beautiful one. Not Christie. Their aunt had always said—

"The others?" That was Gaven's voice. She was almost sure of it. She liked his voice. Maybe he really had found her.

"Ripley and Terrence have everyone aboard. Is she breathing?"

She felt someone touch her forehead, felt a strong hand grab her chin, felt her neck extended.

Christie. Christie. Christie. I didn't mean for you to do it like this.

Her sister's words faded away and Christie let herself float, drifting off into a world of glittering blue water and shimmering bubbles.

The floating sensation and the underwater silence gradually gave way to a tired heaviness, a hard mattress, and the sound of beeping. A regular beeping.

A heart monitor. Like she'd listened to, day in and day out, when she'd worked in the ICU in San

Francisco. The cacophony of ventilators and monitors and alarms blended with the buzz of voices and the bursts of a PA system.

Had she gone back to work? Was she still a nurse?

She couldn't be. She'd quit, hadn't she? She couldn't go back there. Not with all those horrible memories. Memories and sadness.

One voice sorted itself out from the others. She wanted to open her eyes, but she couldn't. And she couldn't understand the words. But, she knew the tone of that voice, the deep reassuring timbre. It was Gaven's voice.

When had she met him?

She tried to remember, but fuzziness coated her thoughts. She heard another voice. A female voice with authority in the words. But the two voices merged together into a babble with no meaning, and the solid weariness pressed against her mind and sent her deeper into a dreamless sleep.

"I've never heard of nitrogen narcosis at a depth of less than a hundred feet," Gaven told the nurse. "We were only at forty-eight feet."

"Yes, it doesn't usually happen during a shallow dive. At least the effects don't become noticeable at that depth. But," the nurse said, "it affects all divers. And you can't predict the depth it will happen."

He knew that. But he'd never seen it before. Not like this.

"We don't know why she's not waking up. Her blood gases showed higher levels of CO_2 than normal—"

"She was shallow breathing on the way up."

"—but her levels are normal now," the nurse finished. "Rapid compression?"

"No, we went down slowly. And we came up slowly."

"So we don't have to worry about decompression sickness."

Good thing. Since Bandit Creek still didn't have a recompression chamber. Any decompression sickness needed to be airlifted to Seattle.

"Nitrogen narcosis usually resolves once you come up. This could be anxiety."

"Anxiety?" She'd been nervous about diving, but not that nervous.

"Besides the impaired judgment, some of the symptoms are visual or auditory disturbances."

He knew that too. Although he hadn't given it much thought. "You mean she could have been seeing things?" Something more than the prank Ripley and Terrence had played when they'd launched that sheet. Things that could have scared her again.

"Maybe," the nurse said. "Sometimes there's giddiness, and sometimes there's extreme anxiety and paranoia. If she was seeing things, and if she was afraid, this could be a hysterical reaction." The nurse thought a moment. "Any known alcohol or drug use? That could make the symptoms worse."

"She didn't seem like she was under the influence."

"Could have been sedative or analgesic drugs. That would affect the narcosis." She consulted the chart. "We've got an emergency contact person from the wallet you brought us. A Meghan McFee. Is that her mother? Or a sister?"

"I don't know." He didn't know anything about her. But he did know she'd been uneasy to begin with. And he should never have taken her down.

"They're trying to call the emergency contact now. Don't worry. Once she wakes up, there won't be any long-term problems." The nurse paused. "Except for . . ."

"Except for what?" He hated it when medical personnel did that. He'd have to remember never to do that when he graduated.

"Except for the occasional amnesia. She may forget everything that happened while she was underwater."

Christie wandered through cloudy images chasing pieces of thought. She saw herself running to catch a cable car. And packing her suitcase without a list. And she saw her aunt standing on the steps in front of the house, screaming at her because she was late. She caught a brief glimpse of her sister, Meghan, stirring a pot of chocolate pudding.

The images overlapped and merged into other images, replaying old parts of her life. She knew she was sleeping and dreaming. Sometimes she surfaced for a few moments and heard the beeping monitor, and then she sank back to oblivion. At one point, she thought someone was holding her hand.

Now she heard the beeping monitor again, such an annoying sound. And then she heard, or dreamt, new voices.

"You look like hell, boy. You been here all night?"

"I couldn't sleep," Gaven said, sounding tired.

An audible sigh. Probably Charlie. "Go get yourself a coffee," he said. "I'll stay with her."

Stay with *her*? Did Charlie mean . . . *her*?

Time crawled on in the quiet room. Quiet except for the incessant beeping of the monitor. She flexed her fingers and realized she could move them . . . and her hands. Just a little.

Her back ached into the hard mattress and her neck throbbed on the stiff pillow. She flexed her fingers again, feeling the life come back into them. And she thought about disconnecting the monitor.

She could disconnect the leads, but that would set off the alarm, and she wasn't ready to wake up.

Or maybe she was. There was light in the room,

she knew that. Not ceiling light, but light from a window. And there was a new sound.

She heard someone snoring.

She opened her eyes and blinked, letting the room come into focus. On her left, a window let in the light of early dawn. She was obviously in a hospital room, with its characterless beige walls. She turned her head to the right, feeling her neck ache, and she saw Charlie, sleeping in an orange plastic chair next to the wall. A woman sat beside him.

Christie blinked again, surprised to see the woman.

She wore little gold-rimmed glasses over intelligent brown eyes. "Good morning," the woman said. And Charlie kept snoring, undisturbed.

The woman looked about forty or fifty or somewhere in between. She wore an old-fashioned dress in a serviceable brown and a huge dark brown hat. She looked like she'd come right out of 1911.

Maybe there was a festival happening in the little town of Bandit Creek. Some kind of frontier days thing.

The woman smiled and nodded her head, and the hat nodded, too. Trimmed with a heap of white feathers, the hat had a deep crown, with a broad drooping brim cocked up on one side.

Shaking out her skirt, the woman stood up. Her

dress was narrow and ankle length, with long sleeves, a wide sash and a stiff collar. She had a lot of wavy reddish brown hair, swept away from her face and gathered into a knot at the back of her head.

After a moment, she stepped closer to the bed. "Are you feeling better?"

Something about the woman's voice sounded familiar. "Who are you?"

"I'm Ethel Hamilton," she said. "I don't live here. I'm just visiting Bandit Creek. I came here to find my daughter, but we missed each other at the train station. And now I'm stuck here."

"Pardon?" Christie couldn't make sense of the woman's words, so maybe this was part of the dream. Although, it felt like she was awake.

"But, oddly enough, I'm starting to like this place, after all this time."

Christie rubbed her eyes and yawned and one of the leads fell off, sending the alarm into a head-aching shriek. Charlie woke up, looking startled. A woman wearing green scrubs calmly walked into the room. She had a blond ponytail, a stethoscope around her neck, and an ID badge that said ICU nurse and her name.

"Look who's awake," the nurse said as she turned off the alarm.

Charlie stood up. Ethel Hamilton sat down again. A man wearing a white lab coat over green scrubs arrived with a clipboard. The pockets of his lab coat bulged with books and notebooks.

"You're probably wondering if this counts as searching for buried treasure," Ethel said, as she leaned back in the orange plastic chair and adjusted her skirt.

What? How could Ethel Hamilton know about that? Had Christie been talking in her sleep?

The nurse shone a light in Christie's eyes. First one, and then the other. "You're in the hospital in Bandit Creek," she said. "You had a diving accident."

"That was no accident," Ethel said.

"You experienced a condition called nitrogen narcosis," the nurse said. "You didn't want to surface. Your boyfriend brought you back up."

"My boyfriend?"

"She means Gaven," Charlie said.

"He's not my boyfriend."

Ethel laughed. "Not your boyfriend, you silly child. He's just the man who saved your life." A little pause. "Well, he helped. Mostly it was me."

Christie glanced at Ethel, and then turned to the nurse. "What is she talking about?"

The nurse smiled, with kind eyes. "What is who talking about?"

"Her," Christie said, looking at Ethel.

"You're still recovering," the nurse said. "You'll feel a little woozy for a while."

Christie ripped off one of the leads, and then the other two. Handing them to the nurse, she said, "I'm all right now. Where are my clothes?"

"You need to take up a different sport than diving." The man with the bulging pockets had been reading his clipboard. His name tag said he was a medical resident. An almost doctor.

"Nonsense. We need to go down there again. As soon as possible," Ethel said, still sitting in the orange plastic chair.

"We need to go down there again?" Christie focused on Ethel. "As soon as possible?"

"Did you hear what I said?" The almost doctor was talking again. "It's not safe for you to dive."

"Never mind him," Ethel said. "He doesn't know what he's talking about. You know how residents are. They think they know everything."

The nurse picked up her light, ready to check pupil reaction again.

Christie pushed her hand away and turned to Ethel. "What do you mean? We have to go *again*?"

"You've gone diving, but you wanted to cross two things off your list while you were here."

"It's not my list."

"Whatever," Ethel said. "Lost Lake is a place you can dive for treasure." She adjusted her skirt and crossed her legs. "You can dive for treasure in lots of places. But you can *find* it here. And it's about time somebody found it."

The nurse wrapped a blood pressure cuff around Christie's arm. "I think she's still hallucinating."

"I'm not hallucinating. I'm talking to her." She waved a hand in Ethel's direction.

Ethel looked amused and indulgent. "They can't see me, dear. Only you can."

Christie felt the world spin as she sank back into the hard mattress. She felt the blood pressure cuff inflating, saw the room darken and heard her sister's voice.

Don't listen to Ethel, Meghan said. *She'll get you into trouble.*

Chapter Four

The next time she woke, brighter sunlight filled the room. It was later in the day, but probably still early morning. Assuming this was the same day.

Someone was holding her hand, again. She opened her eyes and saw Gaven watching her with concern in his dark brown eyes. Beard stubble shadowed his face and his dark hair was tousled. He took his hand away.

She looked at the beige walls and the silent monitor and the rails on her bed. The quiet room contrasted with the chatter in the hallway and the overhead PA system. The costumed woman, Ethel Hamilton, was gone.

A hallucination?

But—Ethel? How had she dreamed up that name? She looked at Gaven, who was still watching her, still with that worried look. "What happened?" she asked him. "We were diving. I remember that. And I saw—"

She stopped, not sure of what she'd seen. Or heard.

He smiled, and he looked relieved. "Nitrogen narcosis," he said. "It's called Raptures of the Deep."

She'd heard of it. "Raptures." She looked into his eyes and wished he'd hold her hand again. If he'd been holding it in the first place.

Maybe she'd imagined that, too.

"It doesn't usually happen unless you're a lot deeper. We weren't that deep." He sounded like he was apologizing.

Of course. It *was* an apology. How stupid she was, thinking he was concerned, about *her*. He was concerned about his reputation. Divers weren't supposed to have accidents. It wasn't good for business.

But, she told herself, it didn't matter. And it didn't matter that her aunt was right. Her aunt had always called Christie a stupid, uncoordinated child. She didn't care. Right now, all that mattered was she had to leave this place. She couldn't be in a hospital.

"I've got to get out of here," she said, a panicky feeling rising inside her. "What time is it?" And then, "Wait a minute. What day is it?"

"It's Thursday. It's the next day. We were

diving yesterday."

Yesterday? It seemed like only moments had passed. And, it seemed like a lifetime had passed. "Where are my clothes? I want my clothes. Now."

"Calm down," Gaven said as he reached for the call bell.

A moment later a nurse appeared. Like everyone else, she wore the standard green scrubs. Her pretty red hair was spiky, her mascara thick, and her earlobes were lined with multiple gold studs. She glanced at Gaven and frowned.

Had he done something to upset the nurse? At least, she could be a nurse. Christie saw the woman's badge and confirmed it. The badge said, Patricia . . . followed by the initials RN.

"Awake? Good." The way she said it, it didn't sound like it was *good.*

Patricia the nurse held up a small flashlight. "Look at me." She checked pupil reaction and then she put her stethoscope in her ears and wrapped a blood pressure cuff around Christie's arm. She inflated it way more than necessary and then slowly let off the pressure.

"Seems normal. A bit low," Patricia said, as she took the stethoscope out of her ears and rewrapped the cuff. "You were hallucinating this morning. Do you have any mental health issues?"

The woman's blunt words hit Christie like a slap. Not a great bedside manner. "No," she answered. She had no mental health issues . . . just a dread of hospitals. And sadness. "Can I go now?"

"The doctor will need to see you. Do you have someone you can stay with?"

"I'm staying at the Lost Lake B&B," Christie said, not answering the question, and cringing at the thought of having to stay in this bed any longer.

"You can't stay alone. You'll have to stay here, so we can monitor you."

"I'll take care of her," Gaven said, as though everything was decided.

The nurse drew a breath, her expression stern, looking like she wanted to disagree. "It will depend on what the doctor says." She stared at Gaven a moment, and then she left.

"I hate hospitals," Christie said. "And I'm hungry. Do you have my clothes?"

"Only what you brought on the boat."

A loose top, shorts, sandals and a wet bathing suit. Wonderful.

The same medical resident from the morning ambled into the room, trailed by Patricia the nurse.

He leaned on the rails, on the opposite side of the bed from Gaven. "Do you remember anything that happened?"

"I . . ." She remembered a lot of things. She just wasn't sure which of them were real.

"The boys were playing tricks," the resident said. "Ripley and Terrence. They probably contributed to your paranoia."

"What paranoia?"

He ignored her question and turned to Gaven. "You talked to them?"

"I did."

"You mean about that sheet? Trying to make it look like a ghost? That didn't scare me."

"It didn't?" The resident sounded disappointed. "I thought that might have set off the paranoia."

"No. I thought it was funny. Isn't that what they were supposed to do? For the ghost town tour?"

She *had* been scared. She remembered that. But she didn't want to get the boys in trouble. They'd meant no harm with their practical joke.

"She was hallucinating this morning," Patricia, the helpful nurse, said.

"Do you remember waking up? Earlier this morning?" the resident asked.

Christie shook her head. "No," she lied, not wanting to give him a reason to keep her in the hospital. "I think I may have been dreaming. Was I talking in my sleep?"

The resident frowned, probably rethinking his conclusions. "You may have experienced some numbness?"

"Not that I remember." And then she thought she'd better give him something. "I do remember a ringing sound."

"Yes, that's a symptom," he said, happily consulting a spiral bound notebook. "And you may have been hallucinating. Hearing things or seeing things. There could have been effects similar to alcohol intoxication. You could have felt anything from," he flipped a page, "excitement to fear."

She had felt that. Both the excitement, and the exhilaration. At first. And then the fear.

"I don't really remember," she said, not wanting to commit to his diagnosis. And not wanting to tell anyone what she had seen. Or thought she'd seen. Or heard.

"It's the loss of focus, and the loss of decision-making ability, and the impaired judgment that are dangerous." He stuffed the notebook back in his pocket and opened the chart at the end of the bed. "Some people can't handle depth. You need to stay away from diving. Is that clear?"

"Yes."

"You may have some other symptoms today. Are you traveling with anyone?"

"She's not," Patricia answered, reporting to the resident. "We can't locate her emergency contact person. The line has been disconnected." She turned her attention to Christie. "Did you know that?"

Of course, she knew. Sadness almost overwhelmed her and she braced, letting the feeling wash through her. "She must have moved."

"Better get a new phone number for her. For now, you'll have to stay here for monitoring."

"You can discharge her," Gaven told the

resident. "I'll stay with her."

"Good. Then she can go." The resident scribbled on the chart. "Keep an eye on her, Gaven. Any more symptoms, bring her back in."

Patricia the nurse had suggested she have a shower, but Christie didn't want to take the time. She went to the bathroom and changed into her top and shorts and sandals. Her hair was a mess, matted from sleeping on it wet. She ran her fingers through it and gave up. There was no one to look pretty for anyway.

And then Patricia insisted that Christie ride in a wheelchair until she was officially checked out. The usual hospital liability issues.

"I don't need a wheelchair."

"If you faint, I don't want to have to deal with it."

"Don't worry. I've got her." Gaven looped her duffel bag over one arm and slipped his other arm around her waist, snugging her against his side. "Let's go."

She didn't need anyone holding her up, but this was preferable to the wheelchair. Not only preferable, but kind of nice.

She shook away the stupid thought. Gaven was still doing damage control for this diving accident. If it really was an accident.

Doubt troubled her thoughts. Maybe

something *had* gone wrong. And maybe not. She knew she hadn't been sleeping well. She'd been traveling too much and she needed rest. And, quite possibly, her doctor had been right. She needed to deal with Meghan.

Gaven opened the door of his truck—an aging pickup truck, white with a lot of rust—and waited until she got in.

"Seat belt?"

She buckled it. He handed her the duffel bag and closed the door. A few minutes later they arrived at the Lost Lake B&B.

From the lane, she could see Mrs. Turnbull, the proprietor, sitting with someone on the patio. All that was clearly visible was Mrs. Turnbull's head with her tightly permed silver hair and her long dangling earrings. The other person was mostly hidden by the rose bushes.

Christie tried to open the pickup door but the latch stuck. In the next moment, Gaven opened it and extended his hand to her.

"I'm all right," she said, not wanting to touch him. Not wanting to imagine things that could not be.

Besides, she didn't need his help. She was perfectly healthy. In mind and body, at least. Maybe not in soul. Maybe her soul would never stop aching.

Gaven took the duffel bag and walked beside her.

As they approached the patio, she could see past the rose bushes and shrubs. Mrs. Turnbull was drinking from a rose patterned china teacup. Her guest sat with her back to the lane. All that Christie could see of the guest was her wavy reddish brown hair, gathered into a knot at the back of her head. On the table, next to the teapot, was her hat. A huge dark brown hat, with a deep crown, filled with white feathers.

Christie stopped walking.

"I've got you," Gaven said.

She felt his arm come around her, and she forced herself to put one foot in front of the other as she moved closer to the patio where Mrs. Turnbull sat with Ethel Hamilton. Ethel still wore her long brown dress with its long sleeves and its high stiff collar. Much too hot for this August day.

Mrs. Turnbull looked up at them, her sharp blue eyes landing on Gaven. "That diving isn't natural. It's not good for a person."

"Hello, Mrs. Turnbull," Gaven said.

Mrs. Turnbull wrapped her plump hands around her tea cup. "You're all right now, Christie?" She set her teacup on the table.

From the little time she'd spent with the older woman, Christie knew her gruff manner was more of a front. She had a take-no-prisoners attitude but under that was a kind heart.

"I'm fine," Christie said, trying not to look at Mrs. Turnbull's guest.

"She's going to have a shower." Gaven kept holding her. "And then I'm taking her out for breakfast."

"You certainly need a shower," Ethel Hamilton said. "You look awful. It's never a good idea to go to sleep with wet hair."

Christie stared at the costumed woman, afraid to say anything.

"Christie?" Gaven leaned his head close to hers. "Do you want to sit down?"

"I'm fine," she said, again, noticing there was only one teacup on the table. Why had Mrs. Turnbull not offered her guest tea?

Maybe Ethel didn't like tea.

"C'mon," Gaven said. "I'll help you up the stairs."

Mrs. Turnbull stood. "You're going up with her?"

"I told the doctor I'd keep an eye on her."

"And I suppose you're going to watch her have a shower?" Mrs. Turnbull said, disapproval in her voice. "I'll make sure she doesn't faint. You go home and have a shower yourself." And then with a slightly kinder voice, she added, "You've been up all night, haven't you?"

He shrugged.

And a touch of hope nudged Christie's tired heart. Maybe Gaven's attentions were not all about damage control.

"Get going," Mrs. Turnbull said. "Come back

in an hour. Then you can take her over to Ma's Kitchen for some breakfast."

Gaven pulled up in front of Ma's Kitchen and parked the truck.

Christie had changed into a gold-colored tank top in some light fabric, and long beige pants that tied at her waist. Over top she wore a loose-knit beige jacket.

The jacket was full of little holes—eyelets—that's what they were called. The eyelets showed the gold underneath. She wore the same sandals as this morning.

Her hair cascaded over her shoulders and her pretty eyes looked wary. Very likely she was afraid of being readmitted to the hospital, because an hour ago at the B&B, she'd looked like she was ready to faint again.

Too bad she hadn't had a successful experience in the water, but at least she could cross diving off her adventure list. If it was the list that had made her do it.

At any rate, whatever she'd been trying to prove, whoever she'd been trying to impress, well, it hadn't quite worked out for her.

Gaven saw Lucy standing behind the counter. As usual, her white hair was coiled in curls, and she was smiling. "Look over there, see her?" He touched Christie's elbow. "That's Lucy. She owns this place with her husband, George. He's the cook." Gaven kept his hand on Christie's elbow, liking the contact. "They're the Grandma and Grandpa of this town."

"I know," Christie said, moving away from him and heading over to one of the booths.

"You do?" He followed her.

"I was in here yesterday for breakfast," she said, and she seemed to relax her guard.

A moment later, Lucy arrived at their booth wearing a red checkered apron. A towel draped over her shoulder.

"Christie, honey," she said, placing a hand on Christie's shoulder. "I'm so glad you're all right. I expect a hospital is the last place you wanted to be on your vacation."

"Nobody wants to be in a hospital, Lucy."

"I know that, honey, but especially not you."

Especially? Gaven wondered what Lucy was talking about. "What do you mean, *especially*?"

"Why, she's a nurse. Didn't she tell you? Even more reason to stay out of the hospital while you're on vacation." Lucy reached in her apron pocket for her order pad. "You two have hospitals in common," she said. "Gaven here, he's almost finished med school. Did he tell you that?"

"No," Christie answered as she read the menu card and avoided looking at them. "He didn't."

Lucy raised her eyebrows, a hint of a smile on her face. "You two should get to know each other," she said, looking at him. Then she turned to Christie. "This fall, he's starting his last year of med school in Seattle."

"I'm not sure about that yet," he said. "I might take a year off."

Lucy frowned. "Just do it, honey. Get it done. You'll make a great doctor. And Bandit Creek needs doctors."

"Thanks."

It was just past eleven o'clock so they were still in time for breakfast. Lucy took their orders for scrambled eggs and bacon and hash browns, and disappeared into the kitchen.

"You're a nurse?"

"I used to be a nurse."

"Used to be?"

"I quit," she said. And then, "Why do you want to take a year off?"

No use trying to impress her. It was pointless. "I can't afford it," he said. "Charlie's paid for most of my med school. I can't take any more of his money."

"Your parents?"

"My father died a long time ago. My mother died when I was sixteen. Charlie is her brother. He took over raising me. I was a tough teenager, so I owe him. For a lot more than money."

"I see."

He didn't see. He'd just told her more about himself than he'd told anybody. Ever. It was like she was a nurse taking a patient history, inviting him to tell her everything that was wrong. He needed to take the focus off himself.

"Who's Meghan McFee?" he asked. "Your mother? Your sister?"

She squared her shoulders and sat up straight. Her wariness was back, and then it dissolved to defeat and her shoulders fell. "She was my sister."

"Was?" *Damn.* He shouldn't have hit her with those questions. "I'm sorry," he said. Yeah . . . that made sense. "That's why the number was disconnected."

"Yes."

"So this was recent."

"Yes. A car accident. A senseless accident."

"All accidents are senseless," he said, wanting to reach out and take her hand. But her hands were in her lap and her face was devoid of emotion, which, he suspected, meant there was a lot of emotion buried inside her.

"Did you take care of her? In the hospital?" She would have. He was sure of it. "Is that why you quit?"

"I don't want to talk about it."

No, she wouldn't want that. Not now. "Well, if you ever do."

Lucy arrived with their orders. "You two having a lover's spat?"

"Lucy." Gaven hoped she'd stop interfering.

"Just sayin', Gaven. Looks like you've got the

girl all upset about something. You need to take lessons from my George. Now go on, say you're sorry. That's always a good start."

"It's not him, Lucy," Christie said. "It's me."

"Oh no, honey, don't you go saying that. You've barely given him a chance. He's quite a charmer once you get to know him."

"Lucy." He sighed. "Go away."

"Just helpin', that's all."

Suddenly, Christie relaxed, and smiled. She'd been beautiful before, but now she was light and radiant, like sunshine moving out from behind clouds.

"That's more like it, honey," Lucy said. "Just give us time. You'll learn to love this town."

Gaven heard the door jingle open and saw Jack enter, looking as haggard as ever. His clothes were ragged but looked clean, and, except for the scruffy beard, *he* looked clean. They probably let him shower at the Community Center. Once the place closed to the regular patrons.

"There's my Jack," Lucy said. "I'd better get him a plate of food."

Christie turned around, looking at the entrance. "Who's Jack?"

"The town drunk," Gaven said. "At least, most of the time he seems drunk. Usually carries a bottle with him, in a brown paper bag. Lucy and George don't let him bring it in here, but they feed him."

"He's homeless?"

"Yeah. I know he sleeps at St. Luke's sometimes, and sometimes at Faith Outreach. And sometimes nobody knows where he is." Gaven swallowed food, almost inhaling it. He hadn't realized how hungry he was.

"He looks harmless," Christie said, in between bites.

"He is, don't worry. He's just a little odd and down on his luck."

Except the man had been down on his luck ever since Gaven had moved here when he was sixteen and that was eleven years ago.

Moments slipped by as they talked about Jack and ate George's home style cooking. When they were almost finished, Lucy approached the table and refilled their coffee cups.

"Looks like a friend of yours just walked in," she said.

He glanced up. Patricia stood near the entrance, no longer in her hospital greens. She wore short white shorts, and a pink and white striped tank top. Odd, that she was here, since it wasn't shift change. With regret, he saw her heading his way. So much for avoiding her.

"Gaven!" she said, with her fake cheerfulness. "Imagine running into *you. Twice* in one day."

"Hello, Patricia." He liked it better when she came out and said what was on her mind. But, most of the time, she didn't. "How come you're not at the hospital?"

She stood at the end of the booth. "I left early." Then she spoke to Christie. "How long have you two been going out?"

Christie blinked, probably blindsided by the intrusive question. "We're not going out," she said. "We only met yesterday."

Patricia looked unconvinced. "I thought, you know, since he was holding your hand while you were sleeping—"

His patience snapped. After the way Patricia had treated Christie in the hospital, he needed to keep the two of them apart. "Excuse us, Christie." He stood up, and grabbed Patricia's arm. "Come with me."

He got her to sit at the end of the counter, far away from the booth where Christie sat with her back to them. Nothing was happening with Christie, and nothing might ever happen, but he didn't need Patricia sabotaging things before they'd even started.

"What are you trying to do?"

"You told me you didn't have time for relationships. Not with you going off to med school. I just think it's odd, you know, that you're already going out again."

"Patricia. I told you—"

"We had a good time last summer, didn't we?"

"Yes, we did," he said.

"And this summer isn't over yet," she said, touching his hand.

. . . . .

Christie sipped the hot coffee, noticing the unique flavor. A hint of chocolate. And then, curious, she glanced over her shoulder and saw Gaven sitting with Patricia at the counter. The nurse from the hospital this morning, with her spiky red hair, her thick mascara and her many gold studs.

Embarrassed, she quickly turned around, hoping Gaven hadn't seen her looking at him. She picked up her fork and began to line up the leftover pieces of hash browns, chiding herself for her wishful thinking.

Patricia had most likely misunderstood Gaven's worry, thinking it was affection, rather than fear of a lawsuit—that explained the woman's abruptness and poor bedside manner. She was obviously his girlfriend.

"She's an ex-girlfriend. They went out last summer when Gaven was home."

Christie felt her chest tighten, and then she let go of her breath, and looked up from the neat rows of hash browns. Ethel Hamilton sat across the table from her, sitting in the place where Gaven had been. Ethel, in her brown dress and her brown hat with all the feathers.

"You're still here," Christie said, setting down her fork and vaguely wondering if Lucy had added something to the coffee.

"Yes, I am."

"You're a figment of my imagination."

"Whatever," Ethel said. "You remind me of my daughter, Annie. She was about your age when she first came to Bandit Creek." Ethel looked off into the distance. "No, Annie was younger than you are. So young. Too young to be setting off on her own."

"Please go away," Christie said, trying to keep her voice low.

"You shouldn't be talking to me. They'll think you're crazy. So just listen."

"Am I crazy?" Christie whispered across the table.

The air hummed and she heard someone else talking to her—inside her head—like a bad phone connection.

You're getting her into trouble.

It was Meghan's voice. The same voice she'd heard this morning in the hospital. The same voice she'd heard yesterday when she'd been diving.

Ethel looked up at the ceiling with a smirk on her lips. "No more than you did. That stupid list was your idea."

What? "You can hear my sister?"

"Yes I can."

"But—"

"Listen to me," Ethel said. "I have a plan, but I need your help."

Her help? Reality wobbled and suspended itself.

All right. So what if this didn't make sense? "Why do you need my help? Why don't you do it yourself?"

"Because, in my present condition, I can't."

Right. Her present condition. Was that a euphemistic way of saying . . . "Are you dead?"

"No," Ethel said, pursing her lips like the idea was distasteful. "Not dead." She thought a moment. "More like recycled."

Christie inhaled deeply and closed her eyes. She definitely needed to stop traveling, and to rest. This was all about exhaustion. She willed herself to relax, and opened her eyes . . . but Ethel was still there. Then Christie looked over her shoulder where Gaven was deep in conversation with his girlfriend.

Or ex-girlfriend, as Ethel had said.

No. Not Ethel. It was her imagination making things up, wanting the world to be different than it was. Even if Gaven were interested in her, she had absolutely no time for a relationship. Not now. Not with everything she had to do. She was out of her mind to even be considering such a thing. They must have given her drugs in the hospital and she was reacting to them.

"You need to listen to me. I have this great idea. It might even work if you don't die in the process."

"Of course," Christie said, wondering if anyone saw her talking to thin air. "As long as I don't die in the process." She picked up the white mug and sipped more coffee. At least the coffee was good, even though her mind was failing her.

"Go to the library and ask to see the old Bandit Creek stuff. They file it under Old Town." Ethel stopped talking, like she was waiting for Christie to agree. "And loosen up, okay? You're so serious."

Just like Meghan used to say. *You're so serious, Christie. Live a little. Do something frivolous.*

"Are you listening to me?"

She didn't seem to have a choice, since she couldn't block out the voice, or the image. "Why me? Why can I see you?"

Ethel gave her a sympathetic smile. "Because you're still holding tightly to your sister, dear."

Of course she was, and she couldn't do anything about it. It was her fault Meghan had died. It's not like she could simply turn off that feeling, wipe the slate clean and continue with her life like nothing had happened.

"Now, here's the thing," Ethel said. "There's been another 'accident' on Lost Lake."

Another accident? Like Christie's so-called accident? Like that diver two weeks ago?

"I know how to stop the accidents and you've got to help me."

No she does not!

Meghan's voice, again. "Did you hear that?"

"Sure. But don't worry. Everything will be all right," Ethel said. Then she added, under her breath, "At least, I think so."

Gaven glanced over his shoulder at Christie. She was doing it again, talking to herself, or arguing with herself. And he made his decision.

"We'll have to discuss this later." He put his hands on the counter and stood up. "I've got to get her out of here."

"Do ya think?" Patricia said, in her normal snippy way. "You know she's hallucinating, Gaven. She had oxygen deprivation. You need to take her back to the hospital."

When he reached the booth, Christie stopped talking and looked up at him, shyly, like she'd been caught doing something wrong.

"We're taking you back to the hospital," Patricia said, sounding as though she had the authority to do that.

"No, we're not. Come out to the park." He reached down and caught Christie's hand, noticing how cold her skin was. And then he heard Lucy, with her Public Address voice.

"Listen up, everybody."

He sat next to Christie, still holding her hand. She shuffled over in the booth making room for him, and tried to pull her hand away. Looking across the table, she focused on the back of the bench.

Patricia stood guard at the end of the booth.

On the other side of the counter, Lucy had positioned herself in front of old Mrs. Templeton, the mother of the reporter, Liz Templeton. The hum of conversation in the diner ceased and they all waited for Lucy's announcement.

"There's been another accident on Lost Lake."

He felt Christie grip his hand. The diner buzzed with anxiety and questions.

"What?"

"Not again!"

"What happened this time?"

"It's just strange, I'm tellin' ya."

"A motorboat," Lucy said. Her hands shook slightly. "It capsized. Father, mother, two small boys. The boys are six years old and three years old."

A chatter of questions followed.

"They'll be all right," Lucy said, clasping her hands. Her knuckles were white. "Fortunately, everybody was wearing life jackets. And, fortunately, Charlie was nearby. He rescued them. They're at the hospital now, being treated for hypothermia."

Lucy picked up a coffee pot and started making her rounds. There was no need for the *Gazette* in this town, news spread on its own.

"Come on, Gaven," Patricia said. "Let's take her back to the hospital."

Christie still gripped his hand as she stared at the empty space across the table. And then, she relaxed. He felt the tension flow out of her, like she'd faced something in herself and made a decision.

"Okay," she said, speaking to the air on the other side of the booth. "You're right. Tell me what I can do to help."

Chapter Five

Gaven stood up, keeping hold of Christie. "Let's go outside," he said, tugging her hand. "There's a park behind the diner."

"I need to go to the library," she answered. But she came with him. "This town has a library, doesn't it?"

He slipped his arm around her waist and urged her past the counter stools toward the back door.

"You need to go to the hospital." Patricia trailed beside them. "You're hallucinating again."

"No, I'm not," Christie said, like this was a friendly conversation. "Just because I'm talking to myself doesn't mean I'm hallucinating. I like talking to myself."

"Nothin' wrong with that." Jack had come out

of nowhere and shuffled behind them, carrying his brown paper bag again.

They exited the back door of the diner and walked into the central town park and the bright August sunlight. A faint breeze rustled the leaves in the branches overhead. A calm, soothing, peaceful sound.

Unlike the sound of Patricia nattering beside him. He needed to get rid of her and get Christie back to Mrs. Turnbull's where she could rest.

"See that bench?" He pointed. "Go sit down."

Christie looked him in the eye, a question forming in her expression. Then she tilted her head as if to say, why not? She left him and walked toward the bench, leaving him to deal with Patricia.

"Can't you see there's something wrong with her? She's talking to someone and no one is there."

Jack stood on the other side of Patricia. "Someone is there, for sure," he said. "But you can't see 'em, missy."

"Go away, you crazy old man," Patricia snapped. And then, "Where did you get that bottle?"

Jack raised his eyebrows, confusion spreading over his weathered face. "What bottle?"

"The one in the brown paper bag, you idiot."

"Oh." The old man looked down at his hand. He clutched the bunched up bag by its neck. "This?" He held up the poorly disguised bottle. "This is from Ripley and Terrence. Nice boys." He nodded and looked off at the middle distance.

"Haven't opened it yet," he continued. "I'm savin' it for somethin' special." He cradled the wrapped bottle and walked to the bench where Christie sat.

With some dismay, Gaven noticed she was still talking to . . . no one. At least he'd got her out of the diner.

"She could be a danger. To herself, or others. Have you thought of that?" Patricia was not letting it go. "Why are you protecting her?"

"Protecting her? From what?"

"You did see her paranoia, didn't you? About staying in the hospital? There are reasons for that, you know. She's probably been admitted before. For psychiatric issues. She can't be wandering around without supervision."

"I'm keeping an eye on her."

Patricia folded her arms and stared at him. "I'll bet you are."

"What's that supposed to mean?" But even as he asked the question, he knew the answer.

She wanted an argument. He shouldn't have said anything. No matter what he told her, she would take his words and twist them to mean whatever she wanted them to mean.

He hadn't known this side of her when they were dating. Or maybe, she hadn't shown it. He reminded himself, again, that it was a bad idea, getting involved in a relationship when he needed to focus on getting through med school. It was best to ignore Patricia.

Jack sat on the opposite end of the bench from Christie and said something to her. She smiled, and reached across the space between them. They shook hands. At least she was talking to Jack instead of thin air.

Gaven let go of a worried sigh. Now that he thought about it, maybe he *was* protecting Christie—from Patricia.

And maybe, he needed to protect *himself* from Patricia. Even though they'd had some fun last summer, by the end of his vacation, he'd had no problem saying goodbye and going back to Seattle. When he'd returned in May, it was Lucy who'd clued him in. Patricia was telling everyone they were still going out. She'd wanted to pick up where they'd left off.

He needed to get out of Dodge.

But first, he needed to help Charlie. And then, he needed to figure out some way to get back to med school. And he wanted to help Christie. She'd lost her sister and she was trying to deal with it.

While he was thinking, Patricia continued to talk at him. Something about drug levels and oxygen deprivation and relapses. Mostly, she was showcasing her critical care knowledge. She enjoyed doing that.

Jack pulled his bottle out of the bag. His trademark bottle of Jack Daniel's.

"We need to find Sheriff Morgan. That drunk isn't supposed to have alcohol in the park."

"He's not drunk. He just ate."

"He's *getting* drunk."

Hopefully not. But he was preparing to twist the top off the bottle. And it did appear to be an unopened bottle because the old man was having trouble unscrewing the cap. He handed the bottle to Christie.

"Oh. My. God. That sick woman is going to open it for him."

Christie accepted the bottle, unscrewed the cap, and handed the cap and open bottle to Jack.

He took the cap, but not the bottle. Then he motioned with an old gnarly hand for her to have a drink.

She looked at the bottle, shrugged, and took a long draft. A few seconds later, she was coughing, and Jack was laughing. Apparently Christie wasn't used to drinking whiskey straight up.

Jack took the bottle and screwed the cap back on. Then he patted her back. She was still coughing.

"Now do you see?" Patricia fumed. "She's as crazy as he is."

With a few quick strides, Patricia reached the bench where Christie, still clearing her throat, sat with Jack.

Patricia knelt down in front of Christie and— using her fake concerned-nurse voice—she said,

"Come back to the hospital with me, dear. They'll give you some dessert. They make really nice chocolate pudding."

As she stared at Patricia, Christie paled. Then she wiped her mouth with the back of her hand and sat up straight. "I hate chocolate pudding," she said, in a level voice. "More than anything in the world."

Patricia's lips thinned to a straight line. She stood, and clutched Gaven's arm. "Yep, she's crazy. You'd better do something about her. Otherwise, I'm calling Sheriff Morgan."

Gaven removed Patricia's hand.

Christie launched to her feet. "Where's the library?"

"The library?" Patricia put her hands on her hips. "What would you want with the library?"

"It's right there." Jack pointed at the old yellow stone building that bordered the park.

This side had one window and a white door. People liked using this park-facing door rather than the Main Street entrance.

A flower box hung from brackets under the tall white-framed window. On each side of the window, wire meshwork held pots spewing various shades of green twirling vines. To the right, more hangers were mounted next to the door, under the lantern-style light, and those pots also held trailing greenery.

The cantankerous old librarian, Mrs. Nancy

Booth, made a better gardener than a librarian.

The upper half of the door featured old-fashioned leaded panes of glass set in three columns of three rows. Below that, were a brass doorknob and a brass mail slot. The slot was supposed to be a book return, but no one ever used it because Mrs. Booth complained about the books dropping on the floor. You needed to return your books during business hours.

A yellow brick patio stretched along the building's edge, displaying a collection of earthenware pots, in various sizes, holding different kinds of plants. Mostly green plants. And a few blooms that looked like daisies, and something dark purple, and some little button-size orange things.

The pots crowded into a haphazard design that ended up looking pleasing. And inviting, even though Gaven often didn't feel welcome in the library.

Mrs. Booth complained at the least bit of noise. But, oddly enough, she let Jack come in, but not for too long . . . and usually only on days when it was raining.

Christie headed along the pathway in the direction of the library.

He followed her. "Why the library?"

"I'm researching the first Bandit Creek," she said. "I believe you call it the Old Town."

"Okaaay. Any particular reason?"

She didn't give him one and kept walking.

He looked over his shoulder. Patricia was crossing the park, heading in the direction of the Sheriff's Office. He blew out a breath and followed Christie into the library.

As they entered, he saw Ripley and Terrence sitting behind the big oak desk to the left of the door. The light from the window fell over the desk, landing on three towering stacks of books and the usual bouquet of flowers Mrs. Booth kept in a green ceramic jug.

"What are you doing?" he asked them.

"Putting new cards in the books," Ripley said.

"Sheriff Morgan gave us community service," Terrence added, unconcerned. "For the sheet incident."

"Quiet in the library!" Mrs. Booth shouted from the other end of the room. Her voice traveled from behind the rows of books.

"Sorry about that," Terrence whispered to Christie. "The sheet. You know, the ghost? We thought it was funny."

"It *was* funny," Christie whispered back. "No harm done."

The boys both looked surprised. "But we thought—"

"The sheet didn't scare me," she said, still whispering. "I had a problem with my equipment. That's why I had trouble coming up."

Gaven pulled her aside and leaned close to her

ear. "It was a problem with *you*. There was nothing wrong with your equipment. I checked it myself."

"It wasn't their fault." Christie looked into his eyes, and he looked right back, noticing the green flecks feathering through the bright hazel.

She turned away from him and looked at the empty space beside her. "It was your fault," she whispered, and—he didn't want to believe it—but it looked like she was talking to no one again.

Okay. He could go along with this. "Talking to your imaginary friend?"

"Yes," she said, turning back to him. "And my imaginary friend is real."

She walked away, heading to the table on the far left wall—where the historical Bandit Creek documents were kept. If it was the Old Town she was researching, she knew where to go. She must have been in here before.

He sighed, wondering what he should do with her. At least, she couldn't get into any trouble reading in here. She might even find it interesting.

Charlie used to come here all the time, looking for material for his tourist speeches. Mrs. Booth gave him all the assistance he needed. Mostly because Charlie had helped with the recovery of some portraits from the Old Town and he'd donated them to the library.

The portraits had been sealed inside a box with beeswax. On one of Charlie's tours, some treasure hunters had found the box and hadn't wanted the portraits since, to them, they had no value. It was Charlie who'd made sure they were donated to the library.

Gaven didn't care about old pictures— professional portraits of distinguished people in the Old Town. He was interested in medicine, not history. And he didn't come to the library often anyway. Although, occasionally he slipped in when Patricia was following him. So far, she hadn't thought to look for him here.

He sat on the edge of the desk where Ripley and Terrence continued checking for full cards and replacing them with blank ones. A notice had been taped to the front of the desk by the Bandit Creek Ladies Historical Society. They were holding an auction to start a fund for a new hospital wing since overcrowding at the Bandit Creek Hospital often sent patients to Missoula.

Good luck with that. It would take a lot of auctions to pay for a new wing. But maybe this would be a start.

He glanced at Mrs. Booth's flowers again. They were bunched together in the green jug and looked like daisies, except they had tighter petals, and some of them were not yet opened. The outer petals were different colors: white, several shades of pink, and a few red ones. All had yellow centers, some light yellow, some darker.

"Do you know what these are called?" He indicated the flowers.

"They're called Straw Flowers." Ripley spoke quietly. "Mrs. Booth thinks they symbolize wisdom. That's why she puts them here," he said. "You know. Like, library equals wisdom?"

"I see."

"Except they don't mean wisdom," Terrence said.

Okay, he thought. "Do they mean anything?"

"They're from the Aster family." Ripley had stopped what he was doing. "Supposed to have healing properties. And they mean love and trust."

"But not, wisdom," Terrence added.

"How do you know?"

"I looked it up on my iPhone," Ripley said. "Don't let Mrs. Booth see you using one of those in here."

Mrs. Booth didn't believe in computers. She said that if people wanted to waste their time playing with the confounded things that was their business, but a library had no use for a computer. At least, not her library.

She did love her check-out cards and she did a good job keeping track of all her books. Each book had a back pocket, holding a card. When you signed out a book, you literally signed your name on the card, and then she got out one of her ink pads and stamped the date beside your name and on the back pocket in the book. She liked stamping the cards. She especially liked stamping them with different colored inks. Some of her ink pads had multi-colors.

With her system, anyone could see a list of who had taken out that book. At least until the card was full, and a new blank card was inserted into the pocket. Which is what Ripley and Terrence were doing now.

Mrs. Booth filed the card, with your signature on it, in a shoe box by due date. If the book wasn't returned within the allotted time, the consequences were severe. No library privileges for a month.

Liz Templeton at the *Bandit Creek Gazette* had once suggested modernizing the system, and she'd been shown out.

"Hey, Gaven?" Terrence shuffled a stack of cards. "Since it wasn't our joke that caused the trouble, do we still have to do this?"

"Yes," he answered. "Keep working."

Christie followed Ethel Hamilton to the long table beside the wall. Bookshelves on either side of the table held different colored boxes with big white labels. Some said GAZETTE, some said DIARIES, and some said PHOTOGRAPHS.

"We need to look at pictures," Ethel said, as she scanned the boxes.

An older lady, probably in her mid-fifties, came out from behind a row of books. She had short curly hair, dyed a dark shade of orange, and little half-glasses perched on the end of her button nose.

She wore a long-sleeved pale pink blouse, a necklace with three strands of flat pink beads, and a dark pink knit vest with large patch pockets stuffed with what looked like recipe cards.

"You're the librarian?"

"Yes, I am."

"I'm Christie Mc—"

"McFee, I know," the librarian said. "You're looking for information about Otto Dredger."

Surprised, Christie felt her mouth drop open. "I . . . Who is Otto Dredger?"

Ignoring the question, the librarian looked at the place where Ethel was leaning down.

As Ethel scanned the labels, her long brown dress puddled on the floor around her and her huge feathered hat brushed against the edges of the boxes.

"Hello, Ethel," the librarian said.

Christie blinked. How—? No way—

Ethel stood and turned around, adjusting her hat. "Hello, Nancy." Ethel smiled. "I like what you've done with your hair. Back in the day, we weren't allowed to color our hair. My, but times have changed."

Jack sat down at the table. His brown paper bag had once again disappeared. No doubt hidden in the folds of his rags.

Feeling lightheaded, Christie sat beside the old man.

"That's Nancy Booth," he said. "Call her Mrs.

Booth. She works here. Practically lives here."

"Please be quiet in the library, Mr. Jack."

Christie glanced over her shoulder at Gaven, sitting on the edge of the desk where Ripley and Terrence were working. A solid oak desk. Gaven looked competent and in charge and . . . real. And Ripley and Terrence were real.

Christie turned back, stared at the empty table in front of her and set her hands on its flat surface. "Am I crazy? Can that librarian see Ethel?"

"Shhh," Jack said. "Pay attention."

"Can *you* see Ethel?"

"I see everything," the old man said.

Mrs. Booth took a navy blue box from the top shelf and set it on the table. "These are pages from the Old Town's *Gazette*." She opened the box. "We have them because some of the fleeing residents took them when they hurried out of the town to escape the floodwaters."

What a strange choice. "Why would they bring newspapers?" Christie asked.

"To wrap a few precious possessions," Mrs. Booth said. "To protect them for travel. They must have stayed packed for some time. There were houses to be built. A whole town to be built. No point in unpacking anything."

Mrs. Booth leafed through the contents of the box. "By the time their treasures were unwrapped, the library had been built. It was one of the first buildings to be constructed after the flood. This building, and the Powder Horn Saloon." Pausing, she shook her head. "Morgan Hawes from the bank donated a lot of money to have the library constructed," Mrs. Booth said. "But we're not interested in him. We're interested in Otto Dredger."

She carefully lifted out a yellowed newspaper article, encased in archival plastic. "Read this," she said. "And this. And here's another one."

Christie skimmed the old pages. The first story concerned a wealthy cattle rancher, Otto Dredger, who was apparently well respected in the Old Town. He was married, with four children: two daughters and two sons. The last son had just been born on Friday, November 24, 1911. The article was dated Monday, November 27, 1911, a few days before the flood that had started on Thanksgiving Day.

At the bottom of the article, there was a note about the date of the holiday that year. President Taft had declared Thursday, November 30, as Thanksgiving Day.

The second article talked about the school needing a new teacher in late October of 1911. The previous teacher had left town for some reason. Otto Dredger was instrumental in attracting schoolteachers to Bandit Creek and had a prominent position on the school board. Not only that, it seemed he and his wife boarded the schoolteachers at their ranch just outside of town.

The last account told something about a dispute between Otto Dredger and another rancher, Luc Branigan. Dredger had accused Branigan of cattle rustling. That article was dated November 10, 1911.

Mrs. Booth walked over to the bookcases. Ethel sat in the chair beside Christie.

"I searched all over town that day," Ethel said. "Looking for my Annie." She took a deep breath, as if remembering something. "One of the young women I talked to was Muriel Hathaway. A barmaid at the Powder Horn Saloon."

"I remember her," Jack said. "Nice girl. She used to slip me scraps."

Christie tried to listen to them. To make sense out of what they were saying. To make sense out of the fact that they were even talking to each other. Or that Jack, who seemed real enough, could see Ethel. And never mind Jack, apparently the *librarian* could see Ethel. Maybe everybody could see Ethel. Maybe—

Christie pressed her fingers into her forehead and squeezed her eyes shut. Maybe she could reboot her brain. But when she opened her eyes, nothing had changed. Jack and Ethel still sat on either side of her, talking about the past like they both belonged there.

Mrs. Booth returned with a bright pink box

labeled DIARIES and set it on the table. She carefully put the newspaper articles back in their box, put the lid on, and moved it aside. Then she opened the new box.

She sorted through several journals, some leather bound, some paper, until she found one with a yellow cardboard cover and tattered pages held together with a frayed red ribbon.

"This is the one," she said, setting the journal on the table in front of Christie. "It was found last year in an attic on Spruce Street. After the owner died, her daughter found this in an old trunk."

Mrs. Booth put the other journals back in the pink box, and then left.

Christie traced her finger over the old cover, feeling the yellow swirls on the embossed paper. Dark and jagged, a crack feathered down the spine for about half its length. The timeworn journal hinted at secrets from a long ago past.

Cautiously, she untied the ribbon and opened the cover to a dedication page. Flamboyant curving lines rimmed a square in the center of the page, showcasing the words written there. Printed words, in careful letters, recorded in a dark blue ink.

Muriel Hathaway, Bandit Creek – Christmas 1901
This book is from Annie Hamilton who taught me my letters.

A drop of ink had stained the page, as the writer had inserted a period after the word *letters*. Enchanted by the childlike printing, Christie turned the page.

Janeary 1, 1902

The writer, Christie was sure, meant *January*. Muriel was learning to spell. Christie's pulse raced. Imagine. This was 1902. It was as if Muriel could speak to the world over a span of more than a hundred years. The first entry said,

Annie told me to write every day.

But Muriel did not write again until—

Febyouary 1, 1902

I am so tired. I work all day.

That was all. Perhaps this was not a child, since she worked. But at the turn of that century, who knew? The next entry said *February 13, 1902*, spelled correctly. The printed letters were neater, and more confident.

Annie is still teaching me. I go to the school after the children leave on Monday and Annie teaches me. We must be careful people do not see me there. It would be unseemly for Annie to be seen with the likes of me.

"What does that mean? Why couldn't she be seen with—"

"That's because she worked at the Powder Horn Saloon," Jack said.

"She was a prostitute?"

"No, not her. She escaped that," Jack said.

On Christie's other side, Ethel fidgeted, making pleats in the skirt of her long brown dress and pressing them with her fingers.

"Muriel Hathaway wasn't a pretty girl," Jack went on. "Plain. Skinny. A big birthmark on her cheek." He looked off in the distance. "Beautiful girl inside though. She was a barmaid. She scrubbed floors by day and served whiskey by night."

More entries followed in March and April. Only a few lines with each entry. One was about her hands hurting from scrubbing. Another told of the jeers from some of the men at the Powder Horn about how ugly she was. One entry mentioned *the kindness of Mr. Jack. He protects me.*

"Mr. Jack? Who is—"

Ethel tapped a finger on the journal and several pages fanned past. "Read this part," Ethel said. "Here's the first mention of Luc."

May 14, 1902

Annie is sweet on the young cowboy Luc Branigan. He brought her daisies to the schoolhouse. She put them in a vase on her desk.

Beneath that entry, Muriel sketched daisies, three of them, each a little larger and more accurate than the last. There wasn't another entry until July.

July 1, 1902

> *I told Annie to stay clear of Mr. Dredger. But how can she? She has to live with his family. He's up to no good. Annie says he is very polite and proper. But I've seen what he does. If only Annie would listen to me. But who would listen to a barmaid.*

Was *Mr. Dredger* the *Otto Dredger* from the newspaper articles? If he was, Muriel's diary suggested a different Otto Dredger than the newspaper had portrayed. Was this man really the upright citizen with the prominent position on the school board?

The next entry was the following day.

July 2, 1902

> *If only Luc Branigan would marry Annie. He loves her. He always has. But Annie won't marry him because she wants to be a teacher. She wants to prove she can be a woman on her own. Silly girl.*

"Why couldn't she marry him *and* be a teacher?"

"If she'd been married, she couldn't be a teacher." Ethel's voice sounded flat, and empty of emotion. Or full of emotion, barely controlled.

"Why not?"

"You couldn't be a teacher and a wife at the same time," Ethel said. "Conflict of interest." She tapped the pages again and they turned to *September 1, 1902*.

In a little part of her mind, Christie realized she was either hallucinating or talking to a ghost who could make the pages turn. But if she was hallucinating, why did Mr. Jack see this too?

And why had she just thought of him as, *Mr. Jack* ... as though he were the man in Muriel's diary?

No. No, she told herself. The Jack sitting beside her and the Mr. Jack that Muriel had referred to—

It was nothing. After all, the librarian had called Jack, *Mr. Jack*.

Christie exhaled, slowly, forcing herself to keep her breathing even. Nothing here could frighten her. And besides, she wanted to read more of the diary. It was not often a person got this kind of glimpse into the past.

September 1, 1902

Mr. Dredger's wife Eliza gave birth to their first child. A little girl. I heard them talking about the child. She is beautiful with bright blue eyes. Maybe Mr. D will pay more attention to his wife now and he will not be following Annie around.

"So you're telling me that Otto Dredger was not faithful to his wife?"

"The diary is telling you that," Ethel said. "I can't tell you anything."

Christie looked back at the yellowed pages and kept reading.

> *October 2, 1902*
>
> *Annie was with Luc Branigan last night. She won't tell me what happened but she looks all happy and nervous at the same time. She says Luc wants to marry her but then she can't be a teacher no more. I think she'll marry him. She loves him.*
>
> *I wish somebody would love me.*

At that moment, Christie felt a chunk of words fall into place. She flipped back to the front of the journal and read the dedication again.

> *Muriel Hathaway, Bandit Creek – Christmas 1901*
> *This book is from Annie Hamilton who taught me my letters.*

Christie remembered. This morning. In the hospital. "This is your daughter? Annie Hamilton is your daughter?"

"Quiet in the library!" The shout came from behind the stacks.

Christie didn't care. So what if she was talking out loud? Maybe even talking loudly? A shiver of reverence filled her as she pressed her hands over the solid pages of the journal. Could it be—?

She turned to Ethel. "You said you came here to find your daughter. When I was in the hospital, you said that. You said you missed each other at the train station. And that's why you're stuck here."

Strong hands gripped her shoulders as Gaven stood behind her. "We have to leave," he said. "Now."

Chapter Six

"But we were just getting to the good part," Ethel said.

"It's that troublemaker, Patricia Patterson." Jack didn't even turn around. He pulled out his bottle of Jack Daniel's and took a swig. Then he offered the bottle to Christie. "Like another drink?" he asked. "You might need it."

"Oh for heaven's sake," Ethel said. "She doesn't need a drink. She needs an explanation."

"For what?" Jack took another long drink and recapped the bottle.

For why she's talking to the two of you, out loud, in the library.

It was Meghan's voice. As clear as if her sister were sitting at the table with them. "Is that my sister?"

"Your sister?" Gaven pulled her up out of the chair. "C'mon, honey. We're leaving. Hurry up."

Ethel. I don't like where you're going with this.

That was Meghan's voice again. Christie stood with her back to Gaven and sucked in a long breath, trying to center herself. To be in the here and now. And as she did, she felt a rising panic. Maybe she really did belong in the hospital.

She looked at the door where they'd come into the library. Ripley and Terrence had left the desk with its stacks of books and were at the window, looking out on the park.

"Patricia is almost here," Jack said. "She's got Sheriff Morgan with her."

Ethel adjusted her little gold-rimmed glasses, then folded her hands and set them on the table. She leaned her head over her hands, forehead furrowed. And then . . . "Tell the sheriff Patricia is jealous."

"Of what?" Jack stared at the label on his bottle of whiskey.

"Of Christie being with Gaven. Can't you see Patricia wants Gaven? The hussy."

Might work. Christie, why don't you kiss him?

"What?" Christie tried to shrug away from Gaven but he caught her hand and spun her around so she faced him. She put her hands on his chest and tried to push him away. He didn't budge. "I have to finish talking to Ethel."

No. She couldn't say that, except she *had* said it, and Gaven couldn't see Ethel.

Images and words swirled through her mind, filling her with confusion. The entries in the diary. Ethel Hamilton really did have a daughter. Jack could see Ethel. Meghan was talking to her.

And Gaven was holding her, urging her to leave this place before that interfering nurse showed up and tried to have her committed.

Christie focused on the buttons on Gaven's shirt. Shiny white buttons on pale blue denim. The top two buttons were open, exposing tanned skin and dark chest hair. He stood in front of her with a tight grip on her shoulders—the only real thing in her life.

As long as you're set on doing my list . . . you might as well kiss a stranger.

"He's not a stranger," Christie said, looking at her hands flattened against Gaven's shirt.

"Who's not? C'mon, Christie," Gaven said under his breath as he pulled her closer. "Snap out of it."

You've only known him since Wednesday morning and it's Thursday afternoon, Meghan said. *That's a little over twenty-four hours. He counts as a stranger.*

"I think it's a good idea," Ethel said. "It can't hurt."

"Might even work," Jack chimed in.

Christie looked at Gaven and saw the concern written over his face. "Kiss me."

"What?" He blinked, surprise registering.

She reached up, placed her hands on Gaven's cheeks and kissed him, her lips lightly touching his.

She was aware of the library door opening, and she heard Ripley say, "Hello, Sheriff Morgan."

And then she didn't hear anything else, except for a sound like a wash of ocean waves, sweeping through her mind. She felt Gaven's hands touch her wrists, pause, and then slide down her arms, and then he was kissing her back. Not like the kiss had begun, but with a yearning and a hunger and a desperation that transported her out of reality. If she had ever been in reality in the first place.

Her world became that little center, standing in the library, with Gaven's arms wrapped around her and her hands slipping into his hair, pulling his mouth tighter against hers. The world spun off kilter, whirling her emotions and scattering her resolve. It could have been seconds . . . it could have been minutes . . . it could have been longer.

Then Gaven lifted his head, but he kept her in the circle of his arms. His dark brown eyes, almost black now, searched hers, looking for . . . an answer? A question? A confirmation? Some kind of evidence that what he was feeling was what she was feeling?

She didn't know. And she didn't care. She watched his eyes, spellbound, unwilling to return to the world. Ready to leave it forever.

Beside them, someone coughed.

Gaven let her go. She imagined light sparkling around her, like a crystal had shattered and the moment was gone.

A uniformed man, about fifty years old, stood next to them. Tall and thin, he wore a taupe-colored Stetson with a brown leather hat band, a taupe shirt with epaulets and dark green pants. A holstered gun attached to his heavy utility belt. The shirt sported state crests at the tops of the sleeves. A plain brass clip decorated his narrow brown tie. And the six-pointed tin star fastened above his heart, if he had one.

His unfriendly expression suggested he didn't.

"Hello, Sheriff. Can I help you?" The librarian had arrived on the scene. Her pink outfit highlighted the rising pink that stained her cheeks. "The latest issue of Model Railroader came in today," she said, smiling, her eyes beaming with admiration. "I set it aside for you."

The sheriff removed his hat, exposing short cropped hair. His expression relaxed. "Hello, Mrs. Booth." The tin star twinkled on his chest. Of course, it wasn't really tin. Nowadays it would be brass. It only imitated the tin stars of the Old West.

"That's her," Patricia said. "She's the one. She's dangerous."

The sheriff tried to resume his unfriendly glare but didn't quite get it right. "The only danger I see is these two making a disturbance in the library." He tried his best to frown at Gaven.

"Gaven. Take it outside."

"Yes, sir."

"And Jack. Put the bottle away."

Jack quickly hid the bottle inside his rags.

"Now, Mrs. Booth, I'd like to see that magazine."

"Right this way, Sheriff Morgan."

They left the library through the door to Main Street, and Gaven glanced back at Patricia. She was standing behind Sheriff Morgan with her arms folded, anger contorting her face. Whatever she'd told Sheriff Morgan about Christie hadn't worked. The sheriff, like everyone else in Bandit Creek, knew Patricia was behaving like a jilted lover.

But why was Patricia so bent on sending Christie back to the hospital? What difference did it make if she was talking to herself? People did it all the time.

Gaven glanced at Christie. She looked like she was listening to a conversation that could only be happening in her head.

He touched her arm. "Christie?"

She snapped back from wherever she'd been. "Thank you," she said.

"For what?"

"For the distraction," she said. "The kiss." She looked at her feet, apparently not wanting to meet his eyes.

"Oh, that." His heartbeat kicked up a notch. "You're welcome," he said. "Anytime."

She turned her head slightly to the right . . . to the empty space beside her. A second later, she spun around and headed down the street.

"Wait a minute." He caught up with her and held her arm to stop her. "Where are you going?"

"I need to see a lawyer." She stepped away from him and kept walking in the direction of the lawyer's office. It seemed she already knew where it was.

"Why?"

She didn't answer, at first, but after a moment, she said, "Why what?"

"Christie!" He matched her pace. "You have to stop talking to yourself like that. At least when you're around people."

"I was talking to Jack," she said.

"Jack is in the library."

"I know."

Okay, she wasn't going to explain. He studied her as they walked, considered for a moment, then decided to say what he thought. "You were talking to your sister." He waited for her to respond but she didn't. "You said, *sister*, when you were in there, remember?"

She'd said another name too. An unusual name. *Ethel*. That was it. "Who is Ethel? I thought your sister's name was Meghan."

"My sister's name is Meghan and I like talking

to her."

They'd reached the Grey Rose Restaurant when she crossed to the other side of Main Street, against the light. Luckily, there wasn't any traffic. He really did need to keep an eye on her.

And she needed to talk about what had happened with her sister because it was eating at her and, he had to admit, maybe it *was* making her a little crazy.

"How long ago did she die?" he asked, trying to keep his voice conversational.

"About a month ago," she said. "The first day of July." She stumbled at the curb and almost fell. But then she got her balance again. "She was making dinner that night. For all of us."

"All of us?" he asked, as they started walking down Spruce.

She seemed focused on something else, like she wasn't paying attention to what she was saying. "Meghan and I lived with our aunt. Meghan's boyfriend was coming over. She wanted to make her special chocolate pudding for him so she went out to get milk." She paused briefly. "To make the chocolate pudding." Her steps slowed.

"And that's when the accident happened?"

"At a red light," she said. "A drunk driver crashed into her car and killed her."

Her words, spoken in a flat tone, filled him with understanding. She came to a stop in front of the Powder Horn Saloon. Her skin had whitened and she clutched her shaking hands together. A single month ago, her world had turned upside down. All because her sister had been picking up last minute groceries and had stopped at a red light. At the wrong time.

He wanted to pull her into his arms and tell her she would get over it. But that would be trite. So he waited, standing in front of her, hoping she'd keep talking. If she could talk about it, she might gradually learn to accept what had happened. But, he knew, she would never get over it. You don't get over losing a sister.

"Where do you think you're going?" Patricia huffed as she caught up with them, winded from running. She positioned herself with her back to the Powder Horn as though she might stop them from entering.

Terrific. Great timing . . . just when he was getting Christie to open up. "I need a drink," he said, mostly to himself.

"Do you think that's wise? Giving her alcohol? In her condition?"

Weariness settled over him and he wondered what had ever attracted him to Patricia last summer. "I'm not giving her alcohol."

Christie stepped between them. "I'm standing right here," she said. "And I'm not sick."

"You're delusional."

"You're not a psych nurse," Christie said. "You work in trauma." She seemed to have recovered, to have stuffed her pain back into a place deep inside of her. She stood with her shoulders straight, her arms crossed.

"I think you're in love with Gaven," Christie continued. "So here he is. Deal with it. I have to see the lawyer." And with that, she marched away and entered the building next door to the saloon. The Law Office of Guiley & Son.

"She needs a lawyer? What's wrong with her?" Patricia squinted, staring at the sidewalk and looking perplexed. "Oh no."

"What do you mean, oh no?"

"She's going to sue you for what happened yesterday."

"No, she's not." Although he had no idea why she'd gone into the lawyer's office and, at this point, he didn't care.

He sat on the end of the wooden bench between the two buildings. Patricia sat right next to him. He sighed.

"You're going to let her? Sue you? Mr. Guiley will—"

"Mr. Guiley's not there," Jack said.

The old man had arrived again, popping out of the blue like he often did. He shuffled over to the bench, clutching his brown paper-wrapped bottle, and sat on the other side of Patricia. She moved even closer to Gaven so that her arm brushed his. Just great.

"That's right," Patricia said. "He's out of town.

Vacation, I think. But he's got another lawyer covering for him. A semi-retired guy."

Jack uncapped his bottle, took a long swig and put the bottle away. "Mr. Lyon," he said. "Nice fellow. From Los Angeles."

"He's from Missoula." Normally Patricia wouldn't talk to Jack, but this was an opportunity to correct the old man and she wasn't going to waste it.

"No, he's all the way from the City of Angels." Jack laughed. "Get it? The City of Angels? Los Angeles?"

"Make him leave, Gaven."

"It's a public bench. He has a right to sit here."

"Nice car that lawyer fellow has," Jack said, unaffected by Patricia's comments.

Gaven had noticed the car a few days ago, and he'd thought it belonged to a tourist until Ripley and Terrence had told him about it.

Parked on the street in front of the Law Office, the shiny 1911 Model T flaunted its stateliness. The antique car had a white canvas roof, dark brown leather diamond tuft seats, and a metallic red paint job.

Ripley and Terrence had interviewed Mr. Lyon and found out the car had an electric start conversion, a two speed rear axle and it could travel at fifty miles per hour.

"Nice wheels," Jack said. "I remember those wheels. They don't make 'em like they used to."

Buffalo wire wheels, with a spare tire behind the running board tool box. Brass headlights and side lights. Brass step plates. Gaven surveyed the car, impressed by the workmanship.

"That thing must cost a fortune," Patricia said. "What is it with men and their cars?"

He wouldn't know. He'd driven a beat-up old truck forever. No surprise, he'd had trouble affording his tuition.

"Takin' her down to the antique car convention," Jack said. "In Missoula. Tomorrow." The old man yawned and closed his eyes.

Ripley and Terrence had also said that Mr. Lyon stayed in character with his car, dressing in period clothing for the time. According to the two teenagers, Mr. Lyon even wore antique wire-rimmed glasses.

"What's she doing?" Patricia asked.

"Signin' papers," Jack said, his eyes still closed.

"What?"

Jack mumbled. Something that sounded like *Trust Fund*.

"Crazy old man," Patricia said. "I wish he'd go away."

They sat in the hot August sun. Jack snored, Patricia attempted small talk, and Gaven waited for Christie to return.

Part of him felt responsible for the dive

accident, but that wasn't why he was here. Another part of him *wanted* to be here, for her.

He knew it didn't make sense to get into a relationship . . . not now. At this point, he didn't even know if he'd be able to return to the hospital this fall.

It didn't matter. This wasn't a relationship anyway.

An hour passed before she came out of the Law Office, looking determined and full of purpose. He still had no idea why she'd wanted to talk to Mr. Lyon.

Or maybe she hadn't talked to the lawyer at all. She'd probably seen the Law Office when she'd driven through town on Tuesday. She'd expect the office would be air-conditioned, and it was. She might have wanted to get away from the heat, and Patricia, and the rest of the world. She could have sat in the waiting room and read magazines for an hour, hoping Patricia would go away.

Unfortunately, Patricia was still here. But the sun's heat was dying down and a slight breeze drifted along the street. He rose to his feet.

So did Patricia. "You're going to sue Gaven," she said.

Christie looked at him. "I'm not going to sue you."

"I wasn't thinking you would."

"I'd like to go back to the library before I commit to this."

"Commit to what?" Patricia couldn't leave it alone. For some reason, she saw Christie as the enemy.

Christie glanced at Jack who was waking up. "Are you coming, Jack?"

He circled his neck, easing out kinks. "Nope. Got to check on things." The old man said it like he had an agenda to follow. "And then I'm goin' to eat at St. Luke's Church."

"You mean, a church supper?" Christie asked.

"Yep. Catholic Women's League. Gettin' money for lab equipment for the hospital. They let me eat for free, providin' I show up for the first sittin'. Five o'clock. Yer welcome to come."

"Maybe we'll go later," Christie answered.

"We?" Patricia's face screwed up with disgust.

Christie turned her attention to Gaven. "Do you want to come to the library with me?"

Sure. Why not. "Don't have anywhere else to be," he said. Other than taking tourists to the bottom of Lost Lake. But he wasn't doing that today. Charlie had canceled the First Time Tour. Tonight, Ripley and Terrence would stay with the boat, and Charlie would lead a night tour.

"I'll go to the library with you," Patricia said, pretending she'd been invited. "You'll need me if she has a psychotic episode."

· · · · ·

Christie sat at the long table where the historical Bandit Creek documents were kept, and Gaven sat beside her.

Patricia took a chair next to the desk where Ripley and Terrence were still putting new cards in the books. Mrs. Booth brought out the box of diaries again. There was no sign of Ethel Hamilton.

Christie turned to the last entry she'd read, handling the fragile pages with care.

October 2, 1902

> *Annie was with Luc Branigan last night. She won't tell me what happened but she looks all happy and nervous at the same time. She says Luc wants to marry her but then she can't be a teacher no more. I think she'll marry him. She loves him.*

> *I wish somebody would love me.*

"Hmm," Gaven said. His arm touched hers as he leaned toward the diary.

"What?"

"They slept together. That's my guess."

"You're probably right. And if she ended up pregnant, it would have been a huge scandal."

They were speaking quietly. Not whispering, but keeping their voices low. There'd been no warning shouts from Mrs. Booth.

They looked at the next entry, written on the following day.

October 3, 1902

Annie says Mr. D took her to the top of his ranch to see the view.

I've heard about that place. Mr. D likes it because he can see everything and he thinks nobody can see him. Stupid man. The Branigans call it Dredger's Ledge. They can see the place across the valley. Anyway, Annie said Mr. D was inappropriate.

This last word was written several times, crossed out, rewritten and finally put down correctly.

"Do you know who Mr. D is?"

"Otto Dredger. A rich cattle rancher."

Annie would not talk about it, but I got her to tell me. She said Mr. D kissed her. How I hate that man.

October 4, 1902

Something is wrong.

"Turn the page," Gaven said.

Christie turned her head instead, watching his eyes. "You find this interesting?"

"I do," he said, looking right back at her. Their heads were close together.

She stared at him. Then she turned back to the

diary, and questioned her sanity for the hundredth time. She had a list of tasks to complete. And a figment of her imagination had added to that list.

But, right now, a handsome and interesting man was sitting beside her and no way was he an illusion. Gaven St. Michel was definitely real, and he was showing at least some signs of being interested in her.

Unless she was imagining it.

Or, unless he really was worried she'd sue him for yesterday's incident.

"In the hospital, were you holding my hand?"

He didn't say yes, and he didn't say no. "I was worried about you."

"Why?"

"You weren't waking up."

But was he interested in *her*? She wanted to believe he was. Wanted to trust her senses. But, considering she'd been talking to a ghost, how reliable could her senses be?

Anyway, it didn't matter. She had a list to complete, and meeting a guy was not on that list.

"It probably had something to do with being tired," she told him. "I've been traveling a lot."

He considered that. "I'll take you down again," he said. "When you're feeling better. A shallow dive. And it'll be a free trip."

"I don't need free. I have a lot of money." She paused for a few seconds. "Meghan's life insurance policy."

There. She'd said it out loud.

He seemed to catch his breath, and to focus more closely on her. Finally, he said, "Did you speak to her? Before she died?"

"Yes."

He waited, inviting her to say more.

She'd had a short time with Meghan at the end, as the confusion of the Emergency Room had buzzed around them. She could still hear Meghan's last words, as clearly as if they were spoken now.

"You know my Life List?"

"Yes, I know, Meg. Don't try to talk."

"Do my Life List for me. Will you do that for me, Christie?"

"Oh, Meg, don't talk like this."

"Promise me, Christie? Do all those things I wanted to do."

Christie blinked and put her hands on top of the journal pages, trying to center herself, until she felt the calm come back. "She had a Life List."

"I thought so," he said, unsurprised.

"What do you mean?"

Gaven lightly set his hand on top of hers. "I had a feeling that diving was not your idea."

"It wasn't," she admitted. "But once I got down there, I liked it."

He smiled. "We could try it again. I'd be happy to take you."

She would like that. And she would like to keep talking, because for the first time since Meghan had died, the words were coming.

"When we were growing up, there was never any extra money. We lived with our aunt. And, I guess I got used to . . . just working." Their aunt had expected it. "Meghan was a year older than me. Somehow she seemed, I don't know, more carefree than me. She always wanted me to . . ."

He waited a beat and then he said, "To try new things?"

"Yes. But I've never had the time. I mean, I've never *taken* the time. And now I feel this need to do her list for her since—"

Another deep breath. Another long sigh. "Well, I feel this need. She wanted me to experience her Life List for her."

"I'm sorry about Meghan."

"It's okay. It seems strange to be talking about her. But it helps, I think."

"Good."

"So far I've had the hot air balloon ride over San Francisco. And I've jumped out of an airplane. Just a tandem parachute jump. I didn't want to take up the sport. Didn't want to take the—"

She caught herself.

"The time," he said.

"Yes."

They were quiet for a moment. Then he asked, "Was one of the things on the list to kiss a stranger?"

She felt her cheeks heat up. "Yes," she said. "It

was."

"We could try that again. I'd be happy to do that too."

She felt herself smiling. She almost wanted to laugh. And she wanted to keep telling him why she was here, while she could still talk about it. In case she never had the courage to talk about it again.

"I read an article online. By a reporter from here, a Liz Templeton, in the *Bandit Creek Gazette*. She wrote about divers. And gold treasure at the bottom of Lost Lake. I thought I could cross off two more things on Meghan's list. That's why I was diving."

"And looking for treasure?" He took her hands and held them. "There isn't any treasure down there, that's a legend. Probably to bring tourists to Bandit Creek." He paused, like he was deciding something. "I suppose we could pretend you're diving for treasure."

"You'll help me?"

"Treasure doesn't have to be gold," he said. "It can be whatever you want it to be." He brushed his thumbs over the tops of her hands. "And I'd like to take you down again. Not deep. We'll go in from the shore. About a mile and a half from the Old Town, along what used to be called Deadman's Gap."

And then Ripley tapped Gaven on the shoulder, whispering. "You'd better take Patricia home. She looks like she's having one hell of a headache."

. . . . .

Christie watched them leave. Just like that, Gaven and Patricia were together again. He'd taken one look at the meddling nurse and gone to her, without a second thought. Patricia had clung to him and he'd put his arm around her and led her out of the library.

Granted, Patricia had *looked* like she was fighting the world's worst migraine, but Christie doubted it. The convenient headache had served its purpose. Patricia had managed to get Gaven to pay attention to her.

It didn't matter. Gaven and Patricia had a history. Christie was an outsider, a tourist who had shown up for a few days.

I wish somebody would love me.

Muriel Hathaway's words in the diary echoed in Christie's mind. What if she was like that woman from a hundred years ago? Fated to watch others fall in love, and never meant to find love herself.

No. Stop right there. She wasn't in love. She'd only met Gaven. Her mind wasn't working. Her life wasn't working. Everything had gone off track since the funeral, and the whole world wasn't working.

Sighing with the futility of it, she looked back at

the pages waiting for her. She'd told Mr. Lyon she would finish the journal entries, so she started reading again.

October 4, 1902

Something is wrong.

Luc walked right past Annie like he didn't know her. I think Luc found out about Mr. Dredger. If only Luc would listen to Annie she could tell him what really happened. But Luc is only nineteen. Just a year older than Annie and me are. Maybe Luc thinks Annie loves Mr. Dredger.

October 15, 1902

Annie is heartbroken. Luc will still not talk to her.

November 1, 1902

Oh heaven help us. Annie is with child. What will she do?

November 2, 1902

I hate Mr. Dredger. Annie told me what he did yesterday. She is distraught.

Muriel crossed out the last word, several times, but she finally got it right.

Annie thought the ride on horseback would do her good. That's why she went with Mr. Dredger yesterday. He gave her something sweet to drink. He told her it would put the health back in her cheeks. Then the next thing she remembered, he had his way with her.

Christie stopped reading. Otto Dredger was worse than she'd first imagined. Hypocritical and cruel. She turned the page, aching for poor Annie and pulled in by Muriel's simple words.

November 7, 1902

Mr. Dredger is angry at Annie. I can tell by the way he acts. I think he knows she was with Luc first. I know he can tell. I don't know how, but men like him, they can tell.

Annie doesn't see the way Mr. Dredger treats her. She is heartbroken. She has no one to turn to. I told her to write to her mother, but she says her mother will not want her. Her mother will be ashamed of her.

"I'm ashamed of myself," Ethel said.

Christie jumped. She should be used to this by now, but she wasn't.

"You didn't know," Jack said.

She startled again. Jack was back too. She wasn't used to the way he popped in either.

"We argued, before she left. I should never have let her leave like that." Ethel sat up straight, adjusted her hat and shook out her skirt. "Keep reading," she said.

Christie looked at Ethel and then at Jack, and then over her shoulder at Ripley and Terrence. The teenagers were no longer putting cards in the books. They were reading them. The light outside the window had changed to a muted light. The glow before a thunderstorm.

Needing to finish what she'd started, Christie turned back to the journal. Muriel Hathaway's next entry was almost three months later.

January 31, 1903

Can hardly believe it. Never thought I would put down these words. Awful awful.

I must write in complete sentences, because Annie said to do it that way. But sometimes the words come so fast, I can't make complete sentences with them.

I will try for Annie.

Annie says she cannot teach much longer because soon someone will find out she is with child. She says Mr. Dredger is bringing a new teacher tomorrow. Annie will live at the ranch. Annie is grateful. She thinks Mr. Dredger cares for her.

Since Mr. Dredger had his way with her, he thinks the baby is his. He will think the baby comes early. If the baby survives at all. Annie is so thin and anxious.

Annie says Mr. Dredger is making his wife Eliza pretend the baby is hers. Eliza already has Maud, only five months old. Poor Eliza has no way of keeping herself or her child. She must agree to the pretending.

Muriel had tried to write 'pretense' but gave up and substituted 'pretending.'

Annie says Mr. Dredger will raise the child and Annie can teach again next September and she can visit the child in secret.

March 1, 1903

I never see Annie no more. She is at the Dredger ranch but the town thinks she went home to her mother. No one sees ~~Eliza~~ Mrs. Dredger either. They will all be surprised when she has a new baby.

June 7, 1903

I sneaked up to the Dredger ranch when I knew Mr. Dredger was at church.

At church? It made sense. Otto Dredger had a reputation to maintain. He was supposed to be an upstanding citizen. He was even on the school board. What a horrible man.

> *Poor dear Annie. She is so sad. Eliza is sad too. At least Mr. Dredger thinks the baby is his so he will do right by Annie and take care of her. I can't tell nobody. Annie is my only friend.*

> *July 7, 1903*

> *The baby was born a week ago. A beautiful baby boy, but he doesn't have the Dredger ice blue eyes. I can't tell nobody.*

> *Sept 1, 1903*

> *There is a new teacher. Now Mr. Dredger says Annie can't be the teacher. He says Annie must work at the Men's Club.*

> *Her life is ruined. She has to pay for the doctor bills. She has to pay room and board for the baby. I told her to write to her mother but she can't. She is ashamed. At least Mr. Dredger thinks the baby is his.*

> *But I know Branigan eyes when I see them.*

"She has to work at the Men's Club?"

"Yes," Ethel said, not elaborating.

Christie searched through her thoughts and remembered. It was in Charlie's story, when they'd been on the boat, going out for that dive. He'd talked about the Men's Club, next door to the Powder Horn Saloon. A high class establishment from the front, but from the back, it was a brothel.

"Your daughter was a prostitute?"

"Not so loud," Ethel said. "You're in a library." The ghost seemed to collect her thoughts, and her dignity. "She was a teacher," Ethel said. "And, yes, she became a prostitute. Because that was the only way she could support herself and her child." Ethel sighed heavily. "It was my fault."

Christie looked at the last lines on the page. They were legible but the ink had been smeared, like water had fallen on the page. Or tears.

Annie helped me learn to read and write. I wish I could help her.

The lights flickered in the library. Ethel reached over and closed Muriel's diary.

Suddenly Mrs. Booth was there. "All done?" she asked.

It seemed like Ethel was done. "Yes," Christie said, handing Mrs. Booth the diary.

The librarian put it back in its box. "Thunderstorm coming in," she said. "We could lose power again." She put the box of journals back on the shelf. "There's one more thing for you to see," she said. "The portraits." She searched along the nearest shelf, scanning the labels.

"Charlie Beauregard found them and donated them. They were preserved in a box sealed with beeswax. There's a portrait of Otto Dredger."

"Did he make it out of town?" Christie asked. "Before the floodwaters rose?"

"There is no record of him surviving the flood." Mrs. Booth walked to the end shelves and bent down, reading the box labels.

"He didn't make it out," Ethel said, speaking quietly so the librarian couldn't hear. "And, it wasn't the flood that killed him. Not really."

"It wasn't the bullets either," Jack said. "They didn't quite kill him."

"No," Ethel agreed. "And it wasn't the fall. But he couldn't move after that, and the floodwaters drowned him. So I suppose you could say the flood killed him." Ethel's mouth flattened in a straight line. "It was a fitting death."

"It didn't make him very happy," Jack said. "That's probably why he's still here."

Christie felt a chill ripple through her body, from the top of her head to the tip of her toes. And then the lights in the library flickered, dimmed . . . and went out.

Chapter Seven

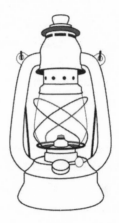

"We're closing," Mrs. Booth said. "Until the power comes back on."

"But, didn't you say I needed to look at a photograph?"

"Not now."

"I'm goin' back to the church before it rains," Jack said. "Just about time to eat anyway and I'm hungry."

"Would you like us to drive you to the B&B?" Ripley asked.

"Yes," she said. "But take me to the Dive Shack. My car is still there?"

"Yes, it is. We can drive it over to the B&B for you, if you want."

"No need, but thanks. I feel fine now. I can

drive."

Thirty minutes later, Christie had her rental car, she'd driven back to town, and she was parked outside the Bandit Creek Hardware & Sports.

"This is the place," Ethel said. "I've seen the divers use those bags. Neat invention."

"You'd think Charlie would rent the bags."

"He does. But only to certain customers. A lot of those treasure hunters were not returning them."

Inside the store, lanterns had been lit, giving the already rustic theme a warm glow and an Old Town feel. They were the only customers. Or rather, Christie was the only customer since the clerk couldn't see Ethel.

But, on second thought, who knew what the clerk could see?

"Ye another one of them treasure hunters?" he asked.

"Not exactly," Christie told him.

"Then what do ye need all these lift bags for?"

"We probably won't need them all." Then, feeling like she needed to give some explanation, she added, "I saw an old bed frame."

He nodded, studying her over the top of his half-glasses. "Ye know the Bandit Creek Ladies Historical Society might object to ye taking it."

"Yes," Christie answered, not prepared for questions. "I mean, um—"

"Don't know why anybody cares about an old

bed frame," the clerk said, as he fingered the price tag on one of the lift bags.

"Of course, I wouldn't take it for myself. I thought it might make a nice addition to the museum."

"Ah, I see. Good." She seemed to pass a test. Then he said, "Taking any rocks?"

"If I find some interesting ones."

"Got a prospector's permit?"

"Yes. I got it today at the Law Office."

"Good." The clerk accepted her credit card. "I'll have to swipe this by hand. No power."

He reached in a drawer and pulled out an ancient manual credit card imprinter. "Ye know how to use 'em?" He set her credit card in the tray. "Tether 'em to the boat," he said. "Ye can shoot 'em to the surface with a few bursts of air." He set the triplicate form in place and swiped the mechanical arm across the plate with a loud clunk.

"These are a favorite," he said. "Most of the treasure hunters like this brand. These keep me in business."

Christie carried the lift bags into the reception room at Mr. Lyon's office. No one was there, not even Mr. Lyon. The town was eerily quiet and empty. The calm before the storm.

Except, it didn't look like it would rain after all. The sun was shining again and the bird sounds had started to return. She could make out the joyful fluting of a meadowlark and she could hear a phoebe saying its name. It was a late Thursday afternoon in the small town, just past six o'clock. Probably everyone had gone home to dinner, or to the church supper.

"All right. That's done," Ethel said. Her little gold-rimmed glasses glinted in the light. "Now we need to get over to Charlie's Dive Shack."

A few minutes later, Christie pulled into the parking lot with Ethel sitting beside her. The ghost had insisted on wearing a seat belt so Christie had strapped her in. Ethel liked seat belts. She thought they were a 'neat' invention. Her tall feathered hat barely fit in the car and the feathers brushed the roof.

"You're sure Charlie will rent to me?" She turned her head to look at the place where Ethel had been sitting. An empty seat now, with the seat belt still buckled.

It didn't look right, having the seat belt done up with no one sitting there, so she clicked the release.

Now what? She had to rent diving equipment, but . . . what if Gaven was here?

She felt a tinge of hope that he would be, followed by a lump of fear. If he was here, he wouldn't let her rent. And she needed to do this dive. If she didn't, she'd never get rid of her ghost.

Sighing wearily, she took a moment to think. It would be all right. Gaven would be with Patricia.

And Charlie would rent her the equipment. The man had been unconcerned about her lack of experience the first time, so he'd rent to her again. He would welcome the money.

When Christie walked into the Dive Shack, Ethel was standing at the counter, a look of disapproval on her face as she watched Charlie.

He sat behind the counter with his feet up on a stool, watching a small television. He was eating a sandwich made of thin white bread and a thick slab of ham. Mustard dripped from the edges.

"Yo! Christie!" He set down the sandwich and wiped mustard off his mouth with the back of his hand. "Feeling better?"

"Much better," she said. Or much worse, depending on how you looked at it. For all she knew, she could be out of her mind. Maybe Patricia had been right.

"Where's Gaven?"

"He's with Patricia."

Charlie's mouth dropped open. "He's what?"

"I need to rent equipment."

He frowned at her, like he hadn't heard correctly. "What kind of equipment?"

"To dive again. Everything I rented yesterday."

He stared at her. "You got a death wish, girl?"

"No. I need—"

"I can't take you down. Not tonight."

Tonight? "You dive at night?"

He blinked, not quite following her. "Sure do.

Nights are real popular. Gives a ghost feeling to the Old Town. Some people like to pretend there are ghosts."

Ethel knocked over his paper clip holder. It was about all she could do. That and turn the pages of a book. She couldn't even do up her own seat belt.

Charlie ignored the paper clip holder.

"You use some kind of lights?" Christie asked.

"Headlamps," he said, pulling one off the rack behind him and setting it on the counter.

"I'll take one of these too."

"No."

"What do you mean, no? I can pay—"

"I can't take you down."

"I'm not going with you."

He'd opened his mouth to say something else, but now he closed it, and he considered what she'd said. "Then who you going with?"

She hadn't expected to be quizzed. "I—"

"Don't even think about it," he said. "In a few days, you can get Gaven to take you on a shallow dive from shore. Nothing for at least forty-eight hours."

"But—"

"No buts. Even if I thought you were safe, which I don't, I wouldn't give you any equipment. Not gonna risk it."

"Nothing will happen to me," she said, automatically.

"To you? Never mind *you*. You might even be

all right. But Gaven would kill *me*."

Christie and Ethel sat on the end of the dock with their legs dangling over the edge. Ethel stared out at the water, her huge hat shading her face from the late day brightness.

The night dive would not leave until sunset, at least another two hours. Bands of clouds stretched across the eastern sky, but the risk of storm had passed. Charlie's dive would go as planned. Christie's would not.

Well, I'm relieved, Meghan said, from somewhere inside Christie's mind. *This was a stupid idea from the start.*

Christie listened, hoping to hear more, but the voice was gone again. Or was the voice simply her own fractured mind? If she was crazy, how would she know?

Exhaustion filled her. She wanted to sleep . . . and to forget about Meghan, and Ethel, and Gaven and Patricia, and the entire world. For a very long time.

"You're not crazy," Ethel said.

Reality thumped back into place and the exhaustion disappeared. All right, she wasn't crazy. For some reason, she could communicate with a ghost. No use trying to make sense of it. It would make sense later.

Or maybe it would never make sense. Maybe

she was just meant to be here at this time.

"Are you going to tell me how the gold got there?"

Ethel looked across the water and after several minutes, she said, "A mine owner was in debt to Otto Dredger. There was a dispute and the mine owner refused to pay. The man was corrupt, like a lot of others, but that's another story."

The ghost smiled, swinging her legs over the glassy water. "I could write a book about all the stories in Bandit Creek . . . if I could hold a pen," she said. "Lots of stories. Everything happens in Bandit Creek."

A fish jumped in front of them and a loon called, off in the distance.

"Dredger decided to take the money in the form of gold. He ambushed the mule train coming from the mine as it came through Deadman's Gap."

"Ambushed?" Did they still *ambush* in 1911?

"Right beyond Deadman's Gap, where the cliff overhung the road to the mine. He dynamited, but he miscalculated. He brought down the whole side of the mountain and blocked the creek."

Dredger blocked the creek? "I thought it was a natural disaster?"

"It wasn't natural."

"And the mule train? It was hit by the rockslide?"

"It was," Ethel said. "Poor mules."

"But, if the gold ore is under the rocks, how can I get at it?"

"You can," Ethel said. "The rock has moved over time. Otto Dredger has uncovered it."

"Otto— Wait a minute." Tingles shivered along her skin. "You mean . . . there's another ghost in Bandit Creek?" Christie liked her ghost. But she wasn't sure if she was ready for another one.

"There are lots of ghosts in Bandit Creek. A lot of souls have not been able to move on." Ethel put her arms behind her on the dock and leaned back. "The creek backed up. Slowly at first. Many left, some dallied. Then the rain came, heavy rain. Heaviest rain to ever hit Bandit Creek, and the town flooded. A lot of people didn't get out alive."

They looked across the water, watching as the light dimmed.

"You didn't get out in time, did you, Ethel."

"No, I didn't. I was looking for Annie."

Poor Ethel. She'd been trying to help her daughter, and Annie probably never knew her mother had come looking for her.

Time edged forward. Ethel didn't say any more. Christie remembered Charlie talking. Was it only yesterday?

"On the boat, Charlie talked about . . . a legend. About the miners who left gold behind. I can't remember what he said, exactly." Because she'd felt scared and hadn't been listening. She had not wanted to dive. Had not thought she could do it.

I remember.

Meghan's voice. Closer now, right beside them.

He said, 'Many have tried to find it. Several have come close. But anyone who tries to take the gold—dies.'

"Well, yes and no," Ethel said with her usual unconcern. "Dredger's been guarding that gold for a long time. He thinks it's his, but it's not."

"Then who does it belong to?"

"It belongs to Bandit Creek. To all the people of Bandit Creek who lost their lives in the flood that he caused." She rearranged her hat. "And, anyway, the curse says that whoever *tries* to find it will die. You won't try, Christie, you *will* find it."

Semantics, Meghan said.

"But even if I do find it, won't he stay with the gold?"

"No," Ethel answered. "Once those nuggets are sold and ground down and scattered like the sands of time, he will have nothing to hold on to."

"And he will leave?"

"Yes."

"So, if I find those saddlebags, is that all of it?"

"As far as we know, that's all of it."

Gaven parked outside Ma's Kitchen. If Christie wasn't here, he was out of places to look. She'd disappeared like she was a ghost.

He should have had Ripley or Terrence drive Patricia home. But the woman had looked so ill, he couldn't say no to her. He'd left her with her roommate. If the migraine worsened, the roommate had promised to take Patricia to the hospital.

That was two hours ago. It was seven o'clock now and he still hadn't been able to find Christie. Worry gnawed at his gut, telling him something was wrong. He had to find her, and soon.

She wasn't at the library, which was closed when he got there. Mrs. Booth would have closed up when the power went off. The power was back on now. It had only been out for a half hour.

After the library, he'd gone to the B&B. Mrs. Turnbull had given him another lecture about the dangers of diving and then she'd told him Christie had not returned.

He'd gone to the dive shack. She wasn't there either, and her car was gone. He'd driven over to St. Luke's, but still no sign of Christie. He'd had to talk to a few people at the church supper and then he'd driven here, to Ma's Kitchen. This was the only other place he could think of. He got out of his truck and walked to the diner. Maybe Lucy knew something.

Christie and Ethel watched the eastern sky across the lake. The sun would set behind them. Reflections from the sun streaked the clouds, turning them orange and purple.

"Those newspaper articles in the library show Otto Dredger as such a great citizen. Didn't the people know what really happened?"

"The sheriff knew, and a few others. But remember, it was—and still is—a small town. Those who knew, what could they say?"

Christie thought about it. Dredger would have had a widow. And children.

"Dredger was dead," Ethel said. "His widow and children needed to be protected. Why tell anyone he was involved in a gold robbery? It didn't change the fact that the gold was buried and lost."

"So they let everyone believe it was a natural disaster."

"That's right. And, until Muriel Hathaway's diary was found last year, anyone researching would only find those newspaper articles." Ethel stopped talking and looked down at the lake. The surface reflected the reverse image of the dock. Impossible to see what was under the water. "Not many people care about the real history," Ethel said. "They care about the legends."

"Hello."

Christie hadn't heard anyone approaching. And now, wonder of wonders, Patricia was coming down the dock, cured of her migraine. "Hello, Patricia."

"I was talking to Charlie," she said. An odd tone colored her voice, making it sound deeper, and thicker. Maybe she was getting a cold? But whatever it was, it didn't excuse her constant prying.

"He said you wanted to dive tonight."

"I did," Christie answered. No use denying it.

"He's being over cautious," Patricia said. "You want to go with Gaven?"

"I—" She wasn't sure what to say to the nosy nurse.

"I rented equipment," Patricia said, smiling. "I put it in your car. You can have my equipment." She turned to go. "Have fun."

"Wait." Christie stopped her. "Why are you helping me?"

Patricia shrugged. "The exercise will do you good," she said, in that thick voice. "It will put the health back in your cheeks."

After a long talk with Lucy, which included several suggestions about how to court Christie, Gaven left Ma's Kitchen by the park door. Lucy had no idea where Christie was. Nor did anyone else in the diner. A growing unease troubled him.

But, maybe he was reading too much into this. Maybe he only wanted to feel like she needed him. She could have gone anywhere for a drive. It was none of his business what she did.

Still, he could not stop worrying.

He heard a crow squawk and he looked across the park. Patricia was sitting on one of the benches near the library. She looked calm. Her migraine was over.

He shook his head. The woman had probably taken a lot of drugs and she should have stayed at her house.

When he reached the bench, she was staring at the ground, looking dazed. No doubt, a lot of medication had been involved. But, how come her roommate had let her leave?

Probably hadn't had much choice. Patricia would have insisted she was well. It was hard to argue with her when she'd made up her mind.

"Feeling better?"

"I feel great," she said.

But her voice sounded raspy, like she was coming down with a cold. She didn't look at him but kept staring at the ground. Something nagged at him.

"You haven't seen Christie, have you?"

Patricia focused on the library, or maybe on something beyond the library, out of sight. "The best thing would be . . . for her to drown."

A chill coated his skin, freezing his bones. "Patricia? Are you all right?"

She squinted at the grass, then she held up her hands and studied them, her expression confused. "I don't think so," she whispered.

. . . . .

Christie sat on the edge of the Zodiac, ready. "I'm supposed to tip backward? Are you sure?"

"That's how I've seen them do it," Ethel told her.

Mr. Lyon said nothing. He cast his fishing line over the other side of the boat, practically oblivious to them. Or her, anyway, since he would not be able to see Ethel. At least, it seemed unlikely that he could see Ethel.

Such a strange man. He was carrying the period clothing a little far, wearing it while fishing. It was the same outfit he'd worn at the Law Office this afternoon when she'd talked to him. At least he'd changed out of his funny shoes and put on rubber boots. But he still wore his antique wire-rimmed glasses. Maybe he thought he'd want to read something while he was out here.

The water mirrored the last rays of the sun. Not even a ripple marred the surface. All was quiet. Not only quiet, but an odd silence had fallen over the lake. The birds had gone away.

The Zodiac floated calmly. Unlike her first trip out, there was no rocking motion to upset her. But she still didn't like the idea of tipping backward.

Ethel was probably right though. There was no way to jump off the boat, so she'd have to let herself fall back off the edge.

She knew the rule about not diving alone, but it wasn't like she was alone, not really, because she had Ethel. And Mr. Lyon.

A small warning pulsed in the back of her mind, but she ignored it. If she didn't do this dive, she'd regret it. Ethel needed her help. And the *accidents* on Lost Lake needed to stop.

Christie had the lift bags and her headlamp, and her BCD was inflated. She put her hand over top of her mask and regulator, leaned back and splashed under the water.

When her body righted and the storm of bubbles dissolved, she held up the air release, tapped it once, cleared her ears, tapped the release again, cleared, and gradually began her second descent to the bottom of Lost Lake.

"Gaven? What did I just say?"

Something very odd, and mean, even for Patricia. "Something about wanting Christie to drown."

"That's what I thought," Patricia said. Her voice was quiet now, and thin. The raspy sound was gone. She stared at her hands, curling and uncurling her fingers. "I think I'm losing it. I think something is wrong with me."

He didn't know what to think. Then he saw Mrs. Booth come out of the library. Now that the power was back on, she was back at work.

She carried a green watering can, but when she saw them, she set the can down beside one of the earthenware pots and waved at them.

No, not *at* them. She was waving *for* them . . . *or one of them* . . . to come over to the library.

"Let's go," he said.

"Where?"

"The library." Christie had been researching in the library. It was unlikely he'd find a clue to where she'd gone, but right at this moment, it was all he had.

"No," Patricia said. She squeezed her eyes shut and pressed her fingers to her temples. "There it is again. My migraine is back."

He took her hand. "C'mon, you can sit in the library. It's getting cool out here anyway."

He doesn't want her to see the portrait.

"What portrait?" he asked as he tugged Patricia toward the library.

"Portrait?"

He could tell she was having trouble concentrating. "You just said something about a portrait."

"No, I didn't. Can you take me home? My head is killing me."

He opened the door to the library and let Patricia go ahead of him.

The portraits your uncle Charlie donated to the library.

"You know about the portraits my uncle donated to the library?"

Patricia looked at him, confusion in her expression. "I don't know what you're talking about, and you're acting weird. Can we leave?"

"The ones they found in the Old Town," Mrs. Booth said. "They were sealed inside a box with beeswax. They're right here."

The lights in the library flickered, though there was no sign of a storm outside. The world was quiet, waiting. Would Mrs. Booth close the library again?

Apparently not. She reached up on a high shelf and took down an old oil lamp. A moment later, she lit it. And then, for the second time that day, the lights went out.

The underwater world blurred and dimmed, even though it was more than an hour before sunset. The headlamp was useful, illuminating about ten feet in front of her.

She concentrated on the rhythm of her breathing, keeping the melody slow and steady, watching her exhaled air bubbles flicker up to the surface.

Finally, she felt her fins touch down on the bottom. The silt whirled up around her, making it even harder to see. About eight feet away, next to a pile of broken trees, she could make out a heap of white rocks. Not exactly white, but glowing, like they were luminescent.

This is the place.

Ethel's voice. Only her voice. There was no sign of the ghost. Was the woman with the long dress and the big hat and the little gold-rimmed glasses still in the boat above? Or was she simply invisible underwater?

My clothes would get all wet.

Of course. What was she thinking. The reality of what she was doing threatened to overwhelm her. So she paid careful attention to the hollow sound of the air coming from the tank, and the whoosh as she exhaled her long, slow breaths.

She adjusted her BCD so she could hover above the floor of the lake. But it was tricky to get it right. She gave up and let her fins rest on the bottom. Then she felt the tremor.

Don't worry. He's trying to keep us away.

No kidding. And better not think about it. All she had to do was attach the lift bags, once she found the gold.

The lake floor shook again and the water wavered, causing the pile of broken trees to tilt and twist. One of the old branches broke off and fell next to the heap of rocks.

Get her out of here! Meghan's voice. *She might die!*

What does it matter? Ethel answered. *Christie keeps saying it was her fault you died.*

No it wasn't!

Yes, Meghan. It was my fault.

Christie didn't know if she was hearing the words in her head, or if she was making them up. It was probably the same thing.

She kicked her fins to swim toward the white

glowing rocks, but an underwater current pushed against her and she could hardly move.

As she struggled, the current grew stronger and stronger . . . until it flattened her on the floor of the lake, pressing her down with a heavy crushing weight.

A little help, Ethel, she thought, wondering if Ethel could *hear* her thoughts.

Christie pulled herself along the bottom with her hands, wishing she had gloves, digging her fingers into the sand, grabbing hold of stumps and half-buried branches, inching closer to the white rocks.

And then she heard Ethel's voice. *They're almost here.*

Who is almost here?

The current let up. The water stilled. She rose off the bottom and started swimming. A few seconds later, the force of the water picked her up and slammed her to the lake floor. She almost spit out her regulator.

Fear invaded her thinking but she pushed it away. She caught hold of a log protruding from the sand, and started counting her breaths. Four beats in, and four beats out.

Once again, the current stopped. She waited, counting, one thousand and one. One thousand and two. Until she got to ten. Not wanting to, she let go of the log. Nothing else happened. She waited a few seconds longer, then tapped some air into her BCD and floated up, about a foot off the bottom.

Straight ahead she could see lights. Not the luminescent rocks, but other lights, flickering into view, and then growing stronger. The nearest moved closer to her. It was a lantern, like a coal miner carried, but it was floating by itself. It had a metal base, speckled with rust, and wire threads encased the glass globe. A thin wire handle extended straight up. And fire burned within the globe. How was that possible?

How was any of this possible?

The lantern moved slightly away from her, and then stopped. She swam toward it, but the lantern moved away again. Then it paused, as if waiting for her. She kept following the lantern until she reached the luminescent rocks. About twenty lanterns hovered in the water all around her, in a large circle.

You'll have to dig in the sand.

She yanked on a small branch, dislodging it from the bottom. The nearest lantern drifted closer, hovering a foot above the lake bottom. She used the branch to dig at the sediment below the disembodied lantern, and after a few swipes, she hit something.

Brushing away the sand with her hands, she touched a smooth surface. Her pulse skittered. *Leather.* The first pair of saddlebags.

Lumpy, ore-filled saddlebags.

. . . . .

Gaven sat at the long table in the library. Patricia sat next to him, holding her head in her hands, moaning. Mrs. Booth placed a black leather folder on the table in front of them and pushed the oil lamp closer.

The light outside the library window had changed to the flat glow before a storm. Was it going to rain or not? Only a little light came in the windows. Not enough to read by. Not without the oil lamp.

He touched the folder and brushed his fingertips over the raised design on the leather. A Scottish thistle. A tiny crack spread along the top edge of the spine. In the lower right corner, stamped into the leather, were the words Tunney Collins. No doubt, the photographer's name. And below that, the date—1910—a year before the flood that wiped out the Old Town.

When he opened the folder, the sepia image of a man stared back at him. The picture was mounted inside and outlined in three bands of silver. The only defect was a smudge on the bottom left of the portrait.

The man looked about forty years old. He had a grim expression, maybe even an angry expression. His narrow scowling face had a closely trimmed beard, and a moustache. His hair was blond and shoulder length, and thinning at the top.

He wore a long gray coat, opened to show a shirt and a string tie, with a vest over top. A gold chain hung from a pocket on the vest. The chain of a pocket watch. He also wore dark pants, a shiny belt buckle and a second buckle, a holster.

The photographer had captured a brooding and surly character. Not a great way to be remembered.

"This is Otto Dredger," Mrs. Booth said.

Beside him, Gaven heard Patricia catch her breath.

"I've seen him," she said. "That's the man I keep seeing."

"Patricia?"

"It's him. I'm sure of it." Patricia's voice was light, almost frantic. "He wants to drown Christie. He's afraid of her. Ethel couldn't hurt him, but Christie can. Oh my God. He's going to drown her."

"Snap out of it," Gaven said, taking hold of her shoulders. "The migraine is making you hallucinate."

"I keep seeing him. He's telling me what to do."

"She's having a migraine," Gaven told Mrs. Booth.

"No," Mrs. Booth said. "She's not. You'd better listen to her."

"Calm down, Patricia." He needed to get her back home, and make sure her roommate kept an eye on her this time.

"You don't understand. I rented diving equipment from Charlie. For tonight's dive."

"Tonight's dive? You're in no condition to dive."

"But you don't understand. I gave it to her."

She wasn't making any sense. "You what?"

"I gave the diving equipment to your friend Christie," Patricia said. "He wants me to get rid of Christie."

Chapter Eight

Otto Dredger may have moved the rocks away, but the lake bed had buried the saddlebags in sediment, preserving them. The sediment protected them from light, and the cold water meant there was little energy for decomposition. The tough leather pouches could have been put here yesterday.

Christie attached the belts from the bright yellow lift bag to the first pair of saddlebags. Then she filled her lungs, took out her regulator and shot a burst of air into the bag. It blossomed and began to lift. She moved it out of the way of the overhanging tree branch, and released it. It hoisted its load toward the surface, rising faster the higher it went, as the water pressure decreased and the air expanded. In half a minute, the lift bag and its cargo disappeared from sight.

Mr. Lyon could reel in the first one. Soon, this would all be over.

Patricia had almost fainted after she'd told him what she'd done. But she'd recovered quickly, and now they stood by the window, watching the hail pelting Ellis Park and destroying Mrs. Booth's carefully tended blooms on the yellow brick patio. Orange and yellow and white and purple petals scattered over the bricks, mixing with pieces of tangled vines.

At least, Charlie would not have gone out yet. The tour was not scheduled to leave until sunset, and the divers knew the trip was weather dependent. The mountain weather was unpredictable. But, would Christie have gone out?

His heart choked. She wouldn't do that.

Would she?

"Christie is stupid enough to listen to Ethel," Patricia said. The raspy quality had come back into her voice. "That's why Ethel picked her."

Ethel? Christie had been talking about someone called Ethel. "Who is Ethel?"

Patricia opened her mouth to say something, and then her face creased in a frown and she looked like she was awakening from a bad dream.

She coughed. "I don't know." Her voice had changed again. Her small voice replaced the harsh raspy sound.

"Why did you give Christie your diving gear?"

"Why—what diving gear? And why would I give diving gear to Christie? Do you think I'm out of my mind?"

Patricia shook her head, as if she were trying to remember something. "Wow. That was some headache. Never had one that bad before."

"You're supposed to be at home. Why are you here?"

"I don't know," she said with some confusion in her voice. Then the confusion left her. Patricia didn't deal with confusion. Not for very long anyway. "I'm better. And I'm hungry," she said. "Let's go over to the diner."

"Can you remember what you were talking about a minute ago?"

"Why are you asking me all these questions? I had a bad migraine. So what?" She took a long breath, a quick exhale, and the subject was closed. "But, you're right," she said. "I didn't tell my roommate where I was going. I'd better text her."

Patricia whipped out her phone. "By the way, does this place have Wi-Fi?"

"Why would I have Why Pie?" Mrs. Booth answered. "Go over to Ma's Kitchen. See if Lucy makes it."

· · · · ·

He'd left Patricia with Lucy and driven straight to the dive shack. Their tour boat, *La Bonne Aventure,* was still at the dock, straining at her moorings and bumping on the floats as waves from the unexpected storm crashed around the vessel.

He got out of his truck, slammed the door and ran for the building. By the time he was inside, he was soaked.

Charlie sat behind the counter with his feet up, eating popcorn and watching TV. Jack sat next to him with his own bowl of popcorn.

"You're still here."

"Of course, I'm still here, boy. Not going out in that storm."

"Did anybody else go out in that storm?"

"Nope," Charlie said, focusing on the TV. "Well—" He frowned.

"Well?"

"The crazy retired guy. I don't think he's back yet." Charlie set down his popcorn and stood up.

"What crazy retired guy?"

"The lawyer," Charlie said, checking the sign-out book. "Semi-retired, I guess. The guy taking over for Mr. Guiley."

"I know who he is."

"From Missoula."

"I thought he was from Los Angeles?" Gaven said. "And what do you mean, crazy?"

"He went fishing in his suit."

"A wet suit?"

"No, his suit. Those old-fashioned clothes he wears so he can look like his old-fashioned car." Charlie stared at the sign-out book and ran his fingers through his hair. "Crap. I think he's still out there."

"He's fine," Jack said, continuing to watch TV and eat his popcorn. "Came in at the dock by the B&B."

"He did?" Charlie and Gaven spoke at the same time.

"He will," Jack said, mumbling around a mouthful of popcorn, still not looking at them.

Gaven hated it when Jack did his incoherent ramblings. He turned back to Charlie. "Have you seen Christie?"

"Yeah, she was in here earlier wanting to go diving. Can you beat that?"

"Did she go out?"

"No," Charlie said. "I didn't rent to her. Hey! Where are you going?"

"Diving," Gaven said. "From shore." Because he'd talked to Christie about doing that shallow dive. Maybe—

"Good idea," Jack said, still with his attention on the TV. "Go to Deadman's Gap."

· · · · ·

You have to hurry. He's creating a storm on the surface.

Christie followed the coal miner's lantern to still another site, dug with her stick until she felt the saddlebag, and then used her hands to uncover it. She attached the lift bag, partially inflated it, and moved it away from the overhanging branches. Then she launched it to the surface and followed the lantern to the next place.

Beside the white rocks, the heap of trees started to shift. They'd been piled there by the landslide. Probably, they always moved a little bit in the lake currents.

She found the next pair of saddlebags and went through the same routine, getting faster at it— attach the cord from the lift bag, give it a burst of air from her regulator, clear the regulator and breathe again. Above her head, a long limb swayed in the current.

Then she noticed the lanterns. Some of them had dimmed. And as she noticed that, she saw one of them flicker out, drop to the floor of the lake and send up a puff of silt.

The storm is washing out of the mountains. He'll swamp Mr. Lyon's boat if we don't hurry.

She had one lift bag left. That must mean there was at least one other pair of saddlebags, right?

More of the lanterns dimmed. Several blinked out. The current grew stronger. Pieces of loose branches lifted off the lake floor and spun in circles in a collection of small whirlwinds. A sandstorm of silt filled the water. More lanterns blinked out, and it was hard to see. Her headlamp only showed what was straight ahead.

We've got the gold. We're done here. Mr. Lyon and I can leave now. What happened to Annie was my fault, but I can leave now.

It wasn't your fault, Christie told the ghost, saying the words in her mind. You didn't know.

The long limb overhead bent and snapped. But a thread of it still clung to the old tree. The currents swirled stronger. All of the lanterns had disappeared.

It wasn't your fault either, dear.

And then Ethel was gone, and the miners were gone, and Christie's air tank was almost empty.

The branch broke off completely and swung around. She ducked, saving herself. But in the next instant, the angry branch crashed down again, pinning her to the lake floor.

Christie knew time moved on, but her will to fight diminished. She inhaled as slowly as she could, conserving what little air remained. The branch leaned, rocked and dropped back, still crushing her as she lay on the floor of the lake.

All of a sudden, a little fish appeared, and something about it was familiar. In the reflection of her headlamp, she saw its green speckled head, its pinkish-red gills, the horizontal pink stripe flashing along its side. Its whispery fins fluttered, as the fish watched her.

You always were the responsible one.

Meghan. Meghan was still with her.

It wasn't your fault, you know.

But . . . it was. Wasn't it?

Sure. Like it was your fault when Mom and Dad died.

I know what you're trying to tell me—

Then listen to me.

The water bellowed like an angry animal and the tree branch pressed down on her, making it hard to breathe. The little fish swam away and Christie couldn't hear Meghan anymore.

But she could hear her aunt—her aunt still haunting her with those long ago words. Her aunt telling her that if she didn't behave herself, her mommy and daddy would not come home.

And they had not come home.

Somehow, in her child mind, she had believed it was her fault. Of course, it wasn't her fault her parents had died. But she'd only been a child, and her aunt had controlled her with threats and guilt.

Aunt Sarah is not a nice woman, Christie. You know that now.

She'd felt the need to do what Aunt Sarah wanted. The need to please the old woman. The need to keep the peace.

Christie had always tried to keep the peace, but now she felt a wash of sorrow for the child she had been, that innocent little child.

And more than anything, she wanted to help that child.

You're not living with Aunt Sarah any longer. In fact, you're getting out of San Francisco.

That's a good idea. She would leave San Francisco. She'd find a job in a new city. With the life insurance money, she didn't even need to work. But she liked being a nurse, she really did. So she'd find a new job . . . in a new city. All she had to do was get rid of this tree.

The current roared all around her, filling the dark water with debris. She twisted to her side, feeling a sharp edge of the branch press against her wet suit. In her hand, she clutched the last lift bag. This is what it was for.

She attached the cord to the tree branch, straining to reach around it. Then she inflated the lift bag with the last bit of pressure from her regulator.

Gaven thought he could see a headlamp. No, *several* headlamps, which didn't make sense. Her headlamp must be reflecting off the rocks. But it was her, he was sure of it. Thank God, he'd found her.

She was rising now. Jack had been right. She'd been at Deadman's Gap. But how had she found this place? And how had Jack known she was here?

As soon as the thought had come, Gaven knew

the answer. It wasn't surprising, not really. She'd developed some kind of rapport with Jack and she'd got him to help her. As usual, the old man knew more than he let on.

There was something beside her, rising with her. Something bright yellow—a lift bag.

Of course, it was a lift bag. She'd been searching for treasure. Crossing things off her list.

Her sister's list.

He swam toward her, reaching her as her head broke the surface. She looked at him, almost like she expected him to be here. He grabbed hold of her vest.

She let go of her regulator and pushed off her mask, oblivious to the water splashing over her face. "It wasn't my fault," she yelled over the wail of the wind.

"Hold on to me," he shouted, taking her hand and guiding it to his vest.

He checked her gauges. She'd cut it close. Her tank was almost empty. He used the remaining air to inflate her BCD.

"It wasn't my fault," she said again, not as loudly.

That her air was gone?

No. It was *his* fault, for abandoning her at the library this afternoon. He should have stayed with her. She'd just come out of the hospital. She wasn't thinking straight, and she wasn't making good decisions.

The waves sloshed over them as they lifted and dropped in the churning lake, holding on to each other. At least the wind was dying down.

"It wasn't my fault," she said, for a third time. "That my sister died."

What? How could she even think that? "Of course, it wasn't your fault." This time he hadn't needed to raise his voice. The wind had stilled.

"Meghan phoned me at work that night," Christie said.

They could have been having this conversation at Ma's Kitchen, instead of tossing in the waves.

"She'd wanted me to pick up some milk, on my way home," Christie said. "But I forgot."

And in some contorted way, she'd blamed herself. "So your sister went out and got the milk."

"Yes."

"And she died."

The lake had calmed. The storm was passing, as quickly as it had started. The sky filled with the reds and golds of sunset. He'd never get used to the crazy weather in the mountains.

"I forgot to pick up the milk," she said again, then paused. Her mouth quirked up on one side, and a moment later, she said, "That sounds silly, doesn't it?"

"At the time," he answered, "it made sense. You wanted to believe there was something you could have done."

A comfortable silence fell between them as they

floated in the water.

"I needed to do this dive alone."

He pulled in a breath, wanting to disagree, wanting to tell her she was wrong, wanting to say the obvious—that you never, ever, dived alone.

And yet, her words made sense. This had been a kind of ritual for her. She'd needed to come out here, alone. "You had me worried."

"Sorry about that."

"From now on, always with a buddy." Then he added, "Preferably me."

"I'm good with that."

His heart swelled and he tightened his grip on her vest. "I'm glad."

The waves lifted them and dropped them in a lulling pattern. The sunset lit the water with a mosaic of color.

"You're all right now? About your sister? It just happened, you know that? You can't blame yourself."

"I know," she said, holding on to his vest and watching his eyes. "Where's your boat?"

"I dove from shore. It was too rough for a boat."

"We're going to be all right," she said.

He wanted to smile. She was trying to reassure *him*.

"You mean, about being stuck in the middle of this lake?"

"These are seven mil wet suits," she said. "They

should protect us for a while."

The yellow lift bag floated about ten feet away. "That's a lift bag," he said. "Find anything?"

"I found all I needed to find. I'm done with treasure hunting and I'm done with Meghan's list." She waited a moment, and then she added, "I'm starting my own list."

He heard the boat motor in the distance.

"Charlie's on his way," he said. "After we get out of here, would you like to go out for dinner with me tonight? The Grey Rose Restaurant? It's a really nice place."

"I'd love to go anywhere with you."

Those beautiful hazel green eyes sparkled back at him. She meant it, he could tell. She liked him.

He wanted to kiss her. He'd wanted to kiss her again ever since she'd kissed him in the library this afternoon. In fact, he'd wanted to kiss her almost from the moment she'd come aboard *La Bonne Aventure*.

The boat would be here in a few minutes, so he took advantage of the privacy and kissed her now, tasting her lips, then deepening the kiss as she kissed him back and wrapped her arms around his neck.

And that's how Charlie found them.

. . . . .

One week later . . .

Gaven could hardly believe his good fortune. His life was full. He'd met Christie and she was all he needed. He still didn't have enough money to go back to med school in the fall, but someday he would.

She'd let go of her sadness and she bloomed with happiness. She was still at the Lost Lake B&B and she didn't show any signs of leaving to go back to San Francisco.

During the day, she went with him on the dive tours and together they explored the Old Town. In the evenings, they built fires on the beach and watched the stars.

He'd told her about his dream to become a doctor and she kept telling him not to give up on Seattle and med school. But at this point, it wasn't a possibility. Not for this year anyway.

"More coffee," Lucy asked, not waiting for an answer as she refilled their mugs. The lunchtime crowd filled the diner. Lucy and her staff were busy.

"I'm glad you learned to love Bandit Creek," she said, speaking to Christie. "Oh, there's Mrs. Templeton." Lucy left their booth and joined the old lady at the counter.

"Who is Mrs. Templeton?"

"She's the mother of the reporter, Liz Templeton. I think old Mrs. Templeton is one of

Lucy's main sources of news. That's why we get the news here first, before it's in the *Gazette*."

"Listen up, everybody." Lucy was speaking in her Public Address voice. "Guess what's in this afternoon's *Gazette*?"

Quiet fell over the diner.

"An anonymous donor has set up a Trust Fund for the hospital. The hospital is getting a Recompression Chamber and a state-of-the-art lab."

A burst of applause and a chatter of questions erupted over the diner as the customers talked about this new development.

"My sister works in that lab," one of them said. "She'll love it."

"What's a recompression thing?"

"It's for the divers. In case there's an accident."

Then someone said, "What they need is more room. My mother had to go to Missoula to get her gallbladder out."

"There will be more room," Lucy told them. "They're building a new wing."

Now there was even more applause.

"That's terrific!"

"About time!"

"Who is this donor?"

Lucy held up her hand. "Anonymous," she said. "We may never find out. But the new wing will be called—the Annie Hamilton Branigan Wing."

More cheers followed and more discussion.

"Branigan?"

"I wonder if the donor is related to our Branigans?"

"Lots of Branigans around here. Their ancestors helped settle the Old Town."

"And there's more." Lucy waited for the diner to quiet again. "There's a scholarship, every year, for any local wanting to pursue a career in the medical field."

There was even more applause, if that were possible. Cheers and whistling and stamping of feet as the population of Bandit Creek felt the joy of this good news.

Lucy waited for the crowd's attention. "And, like the new wing, the scholarship is called the Annie Hamilton Branigan Scholarship. And—" Lucy held up her hand to maintain the quiet. "This year's recipient is . . ." She paused, her face beaming with pleasure.

The whole diner waited in silence. Not even the clink of a teaspoon on a coffee cup. Mrs. Templeton smiled, content to be the bearer of such good news. Finally, Lucy said, "This year's recipient is Gaven St. Michel."

He blinked. He couldn't have heard correctly. "You're kidding?"

"Wouldn't kid about that, Gaven," Lucy said, her voice full of goodwill.

The diner erupted in more cheering. Townsfolk came over to slap Gaven on the back and shake his hand. Christie leaned across the table, for him to hear. "Looks like you're moving to Seattle after all."

He held her gaze, looked into those hazel green eyes. "Only if you come with me," he said.

She touched his hand, watching him. "Then, I think we're both moving to Seattle."

"I think we are," he said, adjusting to the idea. "I think we are."

And so they did.

Carla Roma in the Galapagos

Hello, everyone. I'm Carla Roma and I'm here with Suzanne Stengl, the author of THE GHOST AND CHRISTIE MCFEE. I found Suzanne in the little village of Puerto Baquerizo Moreno on the island of San Cristóbal in the Galapagos Islands. Or as they say here, Las Islas Galápagos.

We're enjoying some ice tea in an open air restaurant beside the ocean and watching the sea lions lazing on the beach.

Carla: I'm glad to finally meet you, Suzanne. Do you have time for a few questions about your upcoming release?

Suzanne: (pouring a pitcher of water over her head . . .) I have all the time in the world.

Carla: It's really hot here, isn't it?

Suzanne: It sure is. Forty-five degrees Celsius. In the shade.

Carla: Whoa. (fanning herself) What's that in Fahrenheit?

Suzanne: You don't want to know.

Carla: I understand you have some pretty authentic details about scuba diving in your book?

Suzanne: Yes, authentic. I've experienced every one of them.

Carla: I'm beginning to understand how hot it would be wearing a seven mil neoprene wet suit in this heat. Do you really need a wet suit? The water doesn't look that cold.

Suzanne: The water temperature here ranges from 64 to 86 degrees Fahrenheit at the surface, depending on the season. Of course, it gets colder as you go deeper. So you need a wet suit.

Carla: If it's as low as 64 degrees Fahrenheit, that's similar to the temperature of Lost Lake, isn't that right?

Suzanne: Yes, it's similar. And in both places, in a wet suit, the temperature is perfect—once you're underwater. It's beautiful. (She looks out at the ocean.) There's a wreck right here, in the harbor.

Carla: A wreck?

Suzanne: A sunken ship. It makes an artificial reef. A place for algae to grow and invertebrates like barnacles and corals and oysters. They provide food for the smaller fish . . . and then the smaller fish in turn provide food for the larger fish.

Carla: (fanning herself) I don't know how the tourists can stand wearing a wet suit until they get in the water.

Suzanne: Most tourists live aboard boats and dive from them. Their sleeping quarters are air-conditioned. (She dumps another pitcher of water over her head.)

Carla: Do the staff care about you doing that?

Suzanne: No, they're used to me.

(The waitress brings another pitcher of water, and another pitcher of ice tea, and sets them on the table.)

Suzanne: Muchas gracias.

Carla: Okay, let's talk about your book. The opening scene in THE GHOST AND CHRISTIE MCFEE has your heroine on a dive boat. And she's seasick. Have you personally experienced that?

Suzanne: I sure have. We did an 8-day tour aboard the Yolita here, in the inner islands, with a group of 16 passengers and 5 crew. Every one of the passengers got sick on the first day. Including Rolf.

Carla: Rolf is your husband?

Suzanne: Yes, he is. He's a traveler.

Carla: You're quite the traveler too, I must say.

Suzanne: No, I'm not. I'm a tourist. There's a difference.

Carla: Then, you're quite the tourist.

Suzanne: I'm the tourist from hell. (She dumps more water over her head.) I should have known I'd get seasick, since I also get carsick, and bus sick, and avoid roller coasters. And like I said, everyone got sick for a day. But since I'm so good at being seasick, I did it for the full eight days.

Carla: That must have been horrible!

Suzanne: Parts of it. Parts of it were great. The food was excellent. Although it would have been even better if I hadn't been so nauseous. And the passengers aboard the Yolita were incredible. Mostly young travelers, all interesting people. The sixteen of us would sit around the big table for meals. For the first few days, French was the default language and then we changed out a few passengers and the default language became English. We had Italian, Swiss, British, Swedes, one guy from California, and the French.

Every day we walked different trails on different islands and saw the endemic plants and animals.

It was a mixed blessing, being on shore. No seasickness, but the heat was extreme. For me, anyway. Before I left the boat, I'd soak my shirt so I could be cool for a time. At the end of the hike,

I'd walk into the ocean. I love my Tilley hat ... because I can dip it in the water and douse my head, when it isn't possible to jump in completely.

Carla: When would it not be possible to jump in completely?

Suzanne: If it was a beach that the sea lions had claimed. They can be territorial.

Carla: (glances uneasily at the sea lion occupying the bench in front of her.)

Suzanne: I don't know why they love those benches, but they do.

Carla: Okaaay ... So, you slept aboard the boat? Weren't you seasick while you were trying to sleep?

Suzanne: Yes. Some nights, when we were making a long open water crossing between islands, it was especially rough. Many of us would lie on the sundeck and watch the stars.

Carla: And that helped the seasickness?

Suzanne: Yes. The stars don't move so they are a reference point. It's like focusing on the horizon in the daylight. And it was fun, lying there with everyone. Kind of like a pajama party.

Carla: Hmmm. But with being so seasick, weren't you afraid you'd be sick while you were diving? That couldn't be good.

Suzanne: It's a real leap of faith, for someone like me—a non-adventurous tourist—to sit in a Zodiac, fully loaded with dive tank, seven mil neoprene and 13 pounds of weights. And feeling nauseous. If you throw up underwater, it's important to keep the regulator in your mouth.

Carla: Eeuw!

Suzanne: Otherwise, you'll drown. But I learned to deep breathe until we tipped over the side. And then all of a sudden, I was underwater and no longer rocking and I was out of the heat. My head was instantly clear and, for about 30 to 40 minutes, life was normal. At least, it was normal for my head and my stomach. The rest of the world was not normal.

Carla: Not normal?

Suzanne: No, it was amazing. Sea turtles, sea lions, penguins, sharks, rainbows of fish. And when we weren't diving, we were snorkeling.

Snorkeling with the little penguins is something I will remember forever.

Carla: Too bad you can't forget about this heat. Can you pass me that water jug?

Suzanne: Sure. Help yourself.

Carla: (dumping water over her head) I'm glad it's not this hot in Bandit Creek.

Suzanne: ¡Yo también!

Carla: Does your heroine Christie McFee get over her nausea and learn to love diving?

Suzanne: You've just read the first chapter so far, right?

Carla: Yes.

Suzanne: Then you'll find out in Chapter Two. More ice tea?

Carla: Please!

About the Author

When I was a child, I shared a bedroom with three of my younger sisters. I used to tell them stories to help them fall asleep. Apparently the stories weren't particularly interesting, because they fell asleep before the stories ended. Unaware that they were sleeping, I would keep telling the story, until my mother called up the stairs. "Sue? They've gone to sleep." And then I would quietly finish the story in my head.

I didn't start writing down my stories until much later. In my last year of university, I collected all the reports from my Marketing Group and wrote up our study like a novel. My classmates liked it, and better, so did the prof.

Finally, after getting a degree in Commerce, I found a little two-line invitation to a romance writers organization in the back of the Writers Guild magazine. And I showed up. I had found my people.

"Suzanne Stengl has a lovely voice with a subtle hint of humor."
—*A.M. Westerling, author of A Knight for Love*

"Suzanne Stengl's descriptions and characters are really memorable."
—*Amy Jo Fleming, author of Death at Bandit Creek*

Dear Reader,

If you enjoyed
THE GHOST AND CHRISTIE McFEE
you can help others find this story
by leaving a short review on Amazon.

Thanks!
Suzanne Stengl

Find more books by Suzanne Stengl here:

Sign up for Suzanne's Newsletter at
www.suzannestengl.com

Made in the USA
Columbia, SC
14 September 2022

67207902R00109